# NON NOBIS

TOM RHYMER

Copyright © 2024 by Tom Rhymer

Published by Flock Publishing, a division of Pink Flamingo Productions

All rights reserved.

No part of this book may be reproduced in any form or by any electronic or mechanical means, including information storage and retrieval systems, without written permission from the author, except for the use of brief quotations in a book review.

Edited by Paige Editorial Services

Formatting by Ebony's Formatting Collective

Cover designed by MiblArt

# Chapter One
## OLIVER

It was morning; Oliver was pretty sure of that. There was light against his eyelids, and the heat that was everywhere in this damnable country was beginning to rise. There was a sound like metal rasping on stone, and it set off a pounding in his brain.

"Blessed Mary, be kind to a dying man," he mumbled as he tried to open his eyes. Something was keeping them stuck shut. Oliver lifted his hand to wipe them clean and discovered that an iron manacle had weighted down his wrist.

*Trouble. You're in trouble, lad. Careful now.*

Cautiously, Oliver moistened his fingers with his lips, softly swore at the pain in his mouth, and rubbed gently at his eyelids, loosening whatever was sealing them shut. They finally opened, and he blinked several times. He sucked at his fingers to wet them again and discovered two things: the stuff sealing his eyelids was blood, and at least two of his teeth were loose in their sockets.

There was a barred gate at one end of the stone chamber,

and light was coming from a tiny, barred window set into the ceiling.

*A cell, then. I wonder what I did.*

There was a moan to his left.

Oliver turned sharply, gasping at the pain in his stiffened joints, and saw a familiar form: Simon, his man—the only one who had joined him on the trip from England. Oliver's father had given all his servants the option to leave with the young lord or remain at home, and Simon had been the only one to step forward.

"Suffering Christ, Simon, what happened last night?" croaked Oliver.

Another moan and the pile of clothing that covered his servant shifted slightly. "There was a fight, milord."

"And we lost, I take it."

"To the Queen's Guard when they arrived," said Simon miserably.

"Bless me." Oliver did his best to check his body for broken bones or wounds, the process somewhat hindered by the heavy manacles on his wrists, secured by chains to an iron ring set into the wall. "And why were we fighting, Simon?"

"You believed the Venetian gentleman was using crooked dice, milord."

"Good reason to fight, then," Oliver mused aloud.

"Perhaps not, given the number of friends the Venetian had with him, milord," offered his servant.

"Hmm." Further speculation was cut short by the arrival of a jailor with a ring of keys. The man unlocked the barred gate and pulled it open, producing a howl of rusted metal that set Oliver's teeth on edge.

"With me, milord," said the jailor, politely enough. Oliver mutely held up his manacled hands. The jailor sighed and stepped into the cell, unlocking the heavy cuffs. Oliver got to his feet and cocked his head. "And my servant?"

The guard shook his head. "My orders are for you alone, milord."

Oliver tensed and prepared to argue the point, but the man stepped back a pace. "Now, Sir Oliver, there's no reason to make this difficult." He nodded towards the cell door, where two other guards waited.

Oliver hesitated, less because of the implied threat than because the jailor had used his name. *They know who I am. That's probably not a good sign.* He sighed, shrugged, and said, "At least make sure my man has something to eat and drink while I am gone." Oliver waited until the guard nodded, then said, "Lead on, my man. Where are we going?"

"The royal court, milord. We are currently in the cells beneath it."

After ascending a set of stairs, Oliver's guards led him to a heavy wooden door set deep into a stone archway. The jailor paused momentarily, then offered, "You may wish to take a moment to rearrange your appearance, milord." Oliver looked down ruefully at the stained mess of his clothing, sighed, and tried running his hands through his hair to give it shape. "Thank you, my man," he said to the jailor, who nodded and swung the heavy door open.

Oliver blinked as he stepped into the royal court's light and bustle. The chamber was filled with sunshine from windows set high into the walls, and the air was filled with the sounds of a dozen conversations as people went about their business. Unfortunately, all the conversations ended abruptly as Oliver was escorted into the room.

"The prisoner as requested, Constable," intoned the jailor, bowing his head.

"Thank you," came the reply from the rear of the chamber. Oliver turned to examine the figure who sat in the high chair on a raised dais, flanked by two chairs to either side, which were currently empty. A splendid and ornately carved wooden rail separated the dais from the rest of the chamber. On the nearer side of the rail were a multitude of people, several of them chuckling and laughing behind their hands at Oliver's sorry appearance. A number of them had gathered into distinct groups. One group was openly scowling at his arrival. Another appeared more sympathetic and included a man Oliver thought looked familiar.

"The prisoner will step forward," said the man in the high seat. He was a thickset fellow in his middle years with a severe look. Oliver did as instructed.

*This could be bad. Ah, well.*

"I am told that you are Oliver of Oakeshott, a man of noble birth from the county of Sussex in England."

Oliver gave a small bow. "Yes, my lord."

The man smiled thinly. "I am William of Bures, Constable to the Kingdom of Jerusalem and Prince of Galilee. You will address me as befits my station."

*Bollocks and bother!*

"Of course, your Highness. My apologies, your Highness."

There were further chuckles from around the room, and one man muttered, "Ignorant lout," just loud enough for Oliver to hear. Oliver turned his head just far enough to fix the man with his gaze and held it. The man stared furiously back at him.

"What are the charges against this man?" asked the Constable.

A well-dressed man separated himself from the knot of men examining Oliver with hostility and bowed to the Constable. "Breaking the Queen's peace, your Highness. Namely, committing an attack upon the person of Bartolomeo de Farrugia, a citizen of Venice."

"And does the accused have an advocate?" inquired Prince William.

Oliver was about to reply negatively when, to his surprise, a man stepped forward from the other knot of people. "He does, your Highness. My name is Pietro Nievolo, a doctor of the University of Bologna."

Surprised murmurs broke out from the crowd, and the Constable's eyebrows rose. "We are fortunate to have such a learned doctor join the court today," he said.

*Who in the nine layers of hell is Pietro Nievolo, and what is he doing here?*

Oliver racked his brains but could not recall ever having met the man or even having heard of him. Even as he did his best to cast a net over his memories, the night before truly caught up with him, and his head began to pound savagely. Oliver tried to follow what was being said by the various figures of the court, but it all seemed to fade into the background of the hammering of his brains.

Finally, there was a moment of blessed quiet. Oliver realized he had closed his eyes against the pain and opened them again, looking around warily. Everyone was staring at him.

"If you could provide the court with an account of your actions last night, Sir Oliver," prompted Pietro Nievolo, who was apparently his advocate for no reason Oliver could comprehend.

"Of course," rasped Oliver, trying to rally. "If it please the court, might I have a drink of water to refresh my throat?" A small titter of amusement made its way through the crowd, although the fellow who had called Oliver a lout made a loud noise of disapproval. He was a burly man with a florid face. Oliver stared at him once more, then took the proffered cup of water and drained it. "My thanks."

"Your Highness, members of the court," began Oliver, gathering his thoughts as best he could. It was not the first time he had been called before a court, although it was usually a member of his extended family who presided and never a prince. "Last eve, I was enjoying the hospitality of the Hanging Grape, a public house in the Venetian quarter. It may be that their hospitality was so welcoming that I overindulged quite unwittingly."

Oliver paused.

*And if you believe that, you'll believe anything. I was sloshed out of my mind and gambling like an idiot.*

When no one contradicted him, he continued. "Unfortunately, this gentleman," he said, indicating Bartolomeo de Farrugia, "took a dislike to me for some reason and began to make negative comments concerning my ancestry and the fidelity of my mother."

"That is a lie!" burst out the angry Venetian. "This fool spilled wine all over my doublet and refused to apologize."

*Your word against mine, chum. We both know I called you out over crooked dice, but neither of us will admit to that.*

"Perhaps," interjected Pietro Nievolo, "in consideration of

the court's time, we can agree that there was a misunderstanding between these two gentlemen—that blows were exchanged—but that no further harm has been done. Sir Oliver is more than happy to make restitution through the payment of a fine and his promise to leave the city of Acre and continue his pilgrimage to the holy city of Jerusalem."

Oliver blinked. *I am?*

Constable William nodded, seemingly content with this arrangement, until he seemed to remember something and raised a hand. "That is all well and good, Doctor Nievolo, but there remains the issue of Sir Oliver's servant, who also struck Master Bartolomeo."

A flash of memory.

*The Venetian merchant lay flat on his back, and Oliver turned to gather his coin from the ground, staggering slightly. The merchant began to rise. Simon gave a warning cry and hurled a pewter goblet into the merchant's face. Oliver looked down to see a thin knife in the merchant's hand. He cursed and kicked the man savagely.*

"My servant was merely seeking to protect me, your Highness," said Oliver.

"And for that reason, he shall not lose his hand," Constable William replied. "Instead, he shall be flogged in the public square. One hundred lashes."

Oliver's body went cold. If a strong hand wielded the lash, that could be a death sentence. "No, your Highness," he said clearly and firmly.

The court went completely still. "I beg your pardon?" asked the constable, his voice rising in disbelief.

His newly found advocate walked swiftly towards him, but

Oliver ignored the man. "I am a belted knight, your Highness. I say that this man Bartolomeo is lying about everything that happened last evening, from first to last. This man provoked a fight and sought to injure me. I struck him down, but my servant did not touch him. I swear this before God. If any man wishes to call me a liar, let him face me in combat and prove it upon my body."

The court exploded in uproar. The advocate whispered fiercely into his ear. "Are you mad? I had you free and ready to walk away. You would risk your life over a servant getting striped?"

Oliver turned and regarded the man coldly. "I do not know you, sir. I thank you for your efforts on my behalf, but I have taken matters into my own hands," he said.

"Ungrateful child!" hissed Pietro Nievolo. "Do you think I did it for your sake? You were acting the drunk and the wastrel and no doubt deserved every penalty the court wished to impose!"

Oliver stared at the man in confusion as the court officers bustled him out of the public chambers and into a private room.

---

By that afternoon, Oliver had managed to get some food and drink into his belly. His head still pounded, and his mouth felt like he had eaten sand, but he no longer felt likely to pass out or vomit. His armour, however, hung on him like a suit of bricks. He could feel the bite of the heavy chain link where the leather padding beneath had worn thin.

*They certainly haven't wasted any time.*

He stood at one end of a dusty field just outside the city. A crowd had gathered to witness what they saw as the day's entertainment. Oliver could only guess at the size of the gathering. Still, he did notice that a tented pavilion had been erected for Acre's eminent nobles to observe the occasion from the comfort of the shade.

*Wouldn't mind some shade myself. I'm roasting out here. Let's get this over with.*

A herald stepped forward from the shade of the pavilion. "Oyez, oyez!" he cried. "On this day, the twelfth of March in the year of Our Lord eleven hundred and forty-four, we stand witness to the judgment of the Almighty God! Before us stand two disputants to the truth, who pledge their bodies as proof of their words, submitting their fates to the Most High!"

The crowd gave an approving murmur.

"On the one side stands Sir Oliver Oakeshott, a knight of England." A few claps, some derisory cheers.

"On the other stands Sir Gerald de Lanier, an officer of the prince's court, acting as champion for the merchant Bartolomeo de Farrugia." Some more enthusiastic cheers.

Oliver squinted as a burly man marched from the tented pavilion. The man wore chainmail, but no helmet, and Oliver easily recognized him from the courtroom as the fellow who had insulted Oliver and called him a lout.

"Oh, good!" said Oliver cheerfully. "I really hoped it would be you."

The herald raised his staff. "The Almighty God shall determine the outcome of this day and show us who bears innocence and who bears guilt. Have the combatants any final words before they begin?"

"I don't like you!" Oliver shouted towards the other knight.

There was a ripple of laughter from the rougher parts of the crowd.

"Insolent English pup! I will redden this ground with your blood!" replied his thickset opponent, drawing an approving cheer.

The herald lifted his staff. Both knights drew their swords. "Begin!" cried the herald, lowering his staff and backing away.

It was over in seconds.

---

In the taverns and public houses that night, experienced soldiers shook their heads as they drank and discussed that afternoon's combat. Whatever Gerald de Lanier's battle experience may have been, he was entirely unprepared for Oliver's swiftness and brutality. The young Englishman, they all agreed, had simply been on another level.

"Almost murder," pronounced one fellow.

"Bite your tongue," said another man scornfully. "Gerald was no innocent lamb. He was armed and armoured, same as the English pup. Anyway, it was all in God's hands, wasn't it?"

There were snorts of laughter, quickly suppressed as the drinkers looked around. "You know the truth of it just as I do," muttered one man, sharp and low. "We all saw that Venetian bastard try his crooked dice. He should have been the one to face off against that Englishman."

"Gerald certainly didn't have to volunteer to act as champion," observed another drinker at the table. "Just didn't like the English fella."

"Dunno why," replied the first man. "That Oliver seemed a friendly enough lad to me."

"Unless you were Gerald de Lanier," offered the second man, and the group chuckled grimly and drank their ale.

---

Oliver leaned against the parapet of the city wall, facing the sea. The tide was coming in, and booming sounds punctuated the slow roll of the waves as they hit the rocks at the base of the wall.

"I spoke too hastily earlier," said a voice behind him. Oliver turned to look at the slender advocate from Bologna, who was half-hidden in the flickering torchlight.

"Perhaps you did, Doctor Nievolo. I am still wondering why you spoke at all. I do not know you," replied Oliver.

"Can you not guess? It's not complicated."

"Ah," Oliver nodded. "You are a tool of my father."

"Tool seems unkind. Let us say that I represent his interests in the Kingdom of Jerusalem."

"I wasn't aware my father had any interests in the Kingdom of Jerusalem," retorted Oliver.

"He does now," replied Pietro Nievolo, with a hint of wry humour.

"Well then, Doctor, perhaps you can tell me what my father could possibly want from me? I have obeyed his wishes. I am here, far away from the shores of England, performing a pilgrimage to the City of God for the benefit of my soul." Oliver made the motion of the cross with his hand.

Nievolo snorted in derision. "Please. You haven't left Acre since you set foot in the Kingdom. The only pilgrimage you've made is to the taverns of the Venetian quarter."

Oliver sighed. "And I shan't be doing that anymore, it seems."

"Not if you value your life. Or that of your servant. People won't like that he got away with striking an esteemed merchant of Venice."

"People," repeated Oliver flatly.

"Well, Venetian people, anyway. Sir Oliver, you must leave the city. You have made it too hot for you," said the advocate.

"I've heard that before," said Oliver.

"Not without reason!" returned Nievolo. "Your father wrote to me regarding how you made the south of England too hot –"

"Is that how he put it?"

"Yes! He told me enough that I can put two and two together and find four," replied the advocate. "You can't fight your way out of everything, for goodness' sake. You are far from home, young man, and outside the reach of your noble sire."

"Apparently not," said Oliver drily.

"I mean, that scandal can touch you here in ways it could not in your father's duchy," Nievolo said.

"Careful, Doctor," warned Oliver, but his tone was light. He raised his hand, and the advocate tensed, but Oliver simply placed it on the man's shoulder in companionable fashion. "I hear you, learned man of Bologna," intoned Oliver, his expression mocking his sombre tone. "I will be a dutiful son and a good Christian and make my pilgrimage to the Holy City of Jerusalem, praying for my soul and the souls of my noble and long-suffering family."

Pietro Nievolo seemed to relax. "I think that will benefit everyone," he said. He made to walk away, but Oliver stopped him by squeezing his shoulder, gripping the advocate firmly.

"Here's a question for you, however. Learned, sir," began

Oliver, "you have some idea of who I am, and you no doubt have a pretty clear idea of what happened last night. Yet God did not strike me down, and I was the victor today. Presumably, this was the will of God. How can that be so?" He peered closely into the advocate's eyes.

Nievolo struggled briefly, but Oliver's grip was iron. The advocate shrugged, wincing as he did so. "Presumably," he managed, "God is keeping you alive for some greater purpose in His plan."

Oliver released the man, who staggered back. The young knight laughed and shook his head. "Make sure my father pays you well," he said, turning, and strode into the night.

---

There was an insistent pushing at Oliver's shoulder.

"Time to be moving, milord," murmured Simon.

"God in His Heaven," grumbled Oliver, rubbing his face. "Why does everyone insist on doing things so blessedly early?"

"So that most things may be accomplished before the full heat of the day, milord."

"Wouldn't it make more sense just to sleep through the whole bloody thing and do everything at night?" he asked peevishly.

"The caravan will be leaving before dawn, milord. It is unsafe for us to travel alone," replied Simon.

"You have an answer for everything, Oh very well, faithful servant. I don't suppose you have any fresh water?"

"On the side table, milord."

"Good man."

A little while later, Oliver emerged from the hostel where

he had rented rooms since his arrival in Acre at the start of the year. The great city's streets were hushed but busy as people took advantage of the cool morning air to do their business. The delicious smell of freshly baked bread wafted down the road.

"Let's buy a fresh loaf for the morning, Simon, that smells divine. Where are we meeting this caravan?"

"Outside the Jerusalem Gate, milord."

"That would make sense. Off we go, then. Are you excited to see the most holy city in Christendom, Simon?"

The servant gave a small smile. "It has long been my dream, milord."

"Well, who would I be to stand in the way of such a thing? To the horses!"

Despite the early hour, Oliver was in a surprisingly good mood. For all his lassitude, leaving Acre and moving on was surely a good thing. He had enjoyed the fast living of a great Mediterranean city, a far cry from sleepy southern England, but, in truth, the delights of the cosmopolitan port had begun to pall somewhat. Getting drunk in Acre was not all that different from getting drunk in Naples, or Marseilles, or half a dozen other places he could name. There should be more to life than just changing backdrops to the same hedonistic routine.

*If only you could hear my thoughts, Father. Such growth!*

The trial by combat had also been a welcome change. There was a rush that came with the risk to life and limb. Oliver was supremely confident in his own abilities and knew that his substantial natural talent had been honed to a fine edge by countless hours of practice and instruction. But one never knew what surprises awaited them in a fight to the death.

"There, milord." They had passed through the Jerusalem gate just as the sky lightened. Simon indicated a substantial gathering of people, horses, pack animals, and carts. The train of humanity stretched far down the road.

"God's wounds, Simon! This isn't a caravan. It's a bloody army!" exclaimed Oliver.

"There is much talk of bandits on the pilgrim road," answered Simon.

"So, is there an escort, or will we all be fighting for ourselves?" Oliver asked grumpily. The thought of sharing a road with this mess of humanity for a week or more had dampened his mood.

"There is a group of knights, milord, who have made it their special duty to keep pilgrims safe on the road to Jerusalem," replied his servant. He gestured to a group of men on horseback, who were keeping themselves separate from the crowd. "Some call them the Poor Knights of Christ or the Knights of the Temple of Solomon. Templars, for short."

"Ah!" Oliver brightened and regarded the group with keen interest. "I've seen them around the city. I would be very interested to see how they fight."

"You may well get the chance, Milord," said Simon.

Oliver steered his horse toward the group of knights, examining them more closely while trying not to make it too obvious. The men wore polished suits of chain mail that still showed evidence of hard use. Over the armour they wore white surcoats decorated with an imposing red cross.

*Good horses, proper armour, quality weapons. These fellows are well prepared for –*

One of the Templars was looking directly at him. For once, Oliver completely lost his composure.

The knight sat in his saddle straight as an arrow. His mail hood was cast back, showing a head of curly black hair. Shining brightly out of the knight's face were a pair of piercing rainwater blue eyes that gleamed with intelligence and humour.

Oliver looked away first, a thing he had never done before.

*Well. It looks as if the road to the Holy City will hold more interest than I would have imagined.*

Oliver smiled to himself for a moment, then frowned.

*Why, in God's name, did I drop my gaze first?*

## Chapter Two
### RUADHAN

He had cursed quietly to himself when the assignments had been handed out in chapter the previous afternoon. Ruadhan didn't mind riding escort on a caravan; that was not the problem. In fact, he quite enjoyed escort duty. It had been the original purpose of the Knights Templar when the King of Jerusalem had given the Order their first charter some twenty years prior. Pilgrim traffic had always been vulnerable to bandits, mostly raiders from the local Saracen lords, although there were some true outlaws among them.

Protecting pilgrims was a right and noble thing and a task which Ruadhan could easily reconcile. That was not the problem. No, the problem was that Gautier de Mesnil had also been assigned as a part of the protective escort.

There were few people Ruadhan despised more than Gautier, although he tried to conceal it given that they shared not only the same Order but were members of the same chapter. He had an intuition that Gautier himself knew of his feelings and that they amused his fellow Templar. If he had been pressed, Ruadhan would have had a hard time articulating exactly why he hated de Mesnil so much, one particular incident notwithstanding. It was just that the smooth-talking Aquitaine knight seemed to be a part of the Order for all the wrong reasons. Which was ironic, given Ruadhan's reasons for joining the Poor Knights of Christ of the Temple of Jerusalem.

Ruadhan shook his head to clear his mind of the thoughts rushing back and forth from one thing to the other. *Such a chaos. Why can I not keep my mind still to focus on a single thing?*

---

It was just before dawn, and Ruadhan walked his horse along the line of people travelling from Acre to Jerusalem. Many of them were travelling on foot, which would slow the pace of the journey.

*A week, maybe a week and a half, if any of them are crippled.*

Ruadhan knew that the possibility of invalids among the pilgrims was high. Many people travelled to the Holy City seeking divine aid for their ailments. He had seen the stacks of crutches, litters, and little wagons resting against the walls of the Church of the Holy Sepulchre.

"A hundred or more, I should say," observed Hugh Thomas, a Welsh brother whose company Ruadhan found easy to bear. Hugh was one of the few who, from the very beginning, had pronounced Ruadhan's name correctly – "Rowan," like the tree. Gautier de Mesnil had laughed and made a joke about the illiterate Irish. Ruadhan had flushed and said nothing, unsure of his position as a freshly initiated brother of the Order. If Gautier had said something like that now, Ruadhan would have broken his teeth, which was probably why Gautier would not have said something like that to his face again. Bullies always knew just how hard to push.

*Damn and blast. I need to stop letting that unctuous slime live in my head.*

"Aye, easily a hundred," replied Ruadhan finally. "Yourself, me, Brother Gautier, and Brother Bernard, plus our sergeants gives us twenty fighting men. The ratio is not bad, but I'm afraid we may still be a tempting target."

"Perhaps we might have a few fighters among the travellers," said Hugh. "That fellow there, isn't he the one who won the trial by combat yesterday?" Ruadhan followed Hugh's gesture and saw a knight talking with his servant. The knight was solidly built and a little stocky – slightly above average height, but with a powerful frame, fresh-faced with a tousled thatch of bright blond hair.

Ruadhan found himself staring, and before he could stop, the knight seemed to become aware of his gaze and locked eyes with him. The fellow blushed, an apple red against his fair cheeks, and cast his eyes down.

Reluctantly, Ruadhan stopped staring at the man and tried to keep his voice casual as he asked Hugh, "So who is this fellow? You said he was in a trial by combat yesterday."

"Ro, did you not even hear about it?" Hugh was incredulous. "It was all a bit of a muddle, but the long and the short of it was that this English knight – Oliver Oakeshott, I believe – basically fought to save his servant from a lashing, if you can believe it."

"He risked his life for his servant?" asked Ruadhan.

"It turned out to be not much of a risk at all. His opponent was Gerald de Lanier, a decent enough fighter in his own way, but the man didn't stand a chance. Oliver over there went through him like a knife through soft cheese."

"A good swordsman, then."

"Better than good, Brother Ruadhan. I don't know if I've seen better," said Hugh.

Ruadhan had to make a conscious effort not to keep staring at the English knight. "Well then," he said, keeping his voice light, "sounds like he'll be a handy fellow to have around if trouble finds us, won't he?"

---

Ruadhan tried to keep his patience as the caravan finally got moving just after dawn broke. A military expedition would have been on the road well before dawn to take advantage of the morning cool, but a collection of pilgrims could not be held to the same standard. Still, Ruadhan had travelled enough in the Kingdom of Jerusalem to know how much of a difference an early start could make. You could only take pilgrims from water source to water source, as they lacked the discipline to make their water stretch. The village of Ma'arat was seven hours on foot, and the last few miles would be thirsty ones in the high heat of the afternoon.

Hugh Thomas and his sergeants were at the head of the caravan, setting the pace. Gautier and his men had the rearguard, which did not please Ruadhan but there was nothing he could do about it. Ruadhan and Bernard were on what they called "shepherd duty" – riding up and down the flanks of the caravan, ensuring that they didn't lose any wanderers or stragglers. It also gave Ruadhan the opportunity to try and gauge the stocky English knight who had captured his attention.

Oliver kept his seat well, his casual riding style the product of hundreds of hours in the saddle. Even the man's servant showed the confidence of an experienced rider. Ruadhan noted with interest that the servant did not ride a mere nag or swaybacked old cart horse but a proper mare with lean muscles under a sleek coat.

Once again, the English knight seemed to feel his gaze and turned to catch Ruadhan staring.

*Damnation!*

Fixing on the first excuse he could find, Ruadhan said, "A fine horse your servant has there."

The knight gave a cheeky grin and replied, "Rosamund? She's a beautiful creature, too much horse for Simon. But when you only have one servant, you make him look as fine as you can." This was accompanied by a most unservile snort from his servant, which undercut his words somewhat.

"You only have one servant?" asked Ruadhan, curious.

Oliver laughed. Ruadhan thought his face looked cherubic when he laughed. "Yes, when I was cast from the shores of England, Simon was the only one who followed, so I suppose I must treat him with reverence, like a house ornament that survives a fire. I'm Oliver, by the way. Oliver Oakeshott."

"Well met, Oliver. My name is Ruadhan Ui Neill." Ruadhan bowed his head slightly.

"And well met to you, Ruadhan Ui Neill!" replied Oliver, only butchering the pronunciation mildly. "A pleasant enough name, although you Irish do seem to have the habit of sprinkling extra letters like salt on a roast." He laughed again. "I'm sorry if I insulted you. I have a habit of not taking myself too seriously, which sometimes spreads to how I treat others as well. There's no harm meant."

"No harm taken," replied Ruadhan, surprised and gratified at how easy the Englishman was to talk to. Ruadhan was often stiff and remote in conversation and could take a while to warm up. Oliver's easy manner was quite disarming.

"So how on Earth does a fighting man from far-flung Ireland end up joining the Knights Templar?" asked Oliver.

Ruadhan did not want to tell the usual lie, and there was no way he could possibly tell the truth to this man he had just met. "Let us call it a recovery from misfortune," he said, which was not technically untrue, then changed the subject. "And how does a fighting man from far-flung England end up on the shores of the Kingdom of Jerusalem?"

"Oh, my story is definitely a recovery from misfortune as well, only in my case, the misfortunes are always my bloody fault," replied Oliver, laughing once again. "I have a long and storied history of being the architect of my own downfall, my young years notwithstanding."

"Well, if you get yourself into trouble, you seem quite capable of getting yourself out again," observed Ruadhan.

Mischief gleamed in Oliver's green eyes. "You saw the trial by combat, then."

"I did not. I hear that I missed quite the display."

"Flattery, Sir Ruadhan Ui Neill, will get you nowhere," said Oliver, glancing sideways at Ruadhan.

"And gambling will find you a place on a pilgrim's road to Jerusalem," replied Ruadhan, a little rattled.

"Oh, so the real story is out!" laughed Oliver, slapping the Irish knight on his mailed shoulder. Ruadhan was a little surprised by the familiar touch but found that he didn't mind it. "Thank heavens. Although be careful, Ruadhan. I swore an oath before God that the Venetian attacked me without provocation, and God guided my sword in the trial that followed. So clearly, I must have been telling the truth, or are you saying God was wrong?"

"My time in the Kingdom has taught me that God moves in mysterious ways," answered Ruadhan drily. "I heard about what happened to the Venetian's champion, Gerald de Lanier, but what happened to the Venetian himself?"

"Bartolomeo? I've no idea," said Oliver, looking surprised. "Something rather nasty, I suppose."

---

Ruadhan made his excuses and continued his duty as a shepherd of pilgrims, but his thoughts were entirely upon Oliver. The English knight practically bubbled over with life, wit, and humour. It was extraordinary, and it had a powerful effect on Ruadhan. Somehow, life seemed less serious and grim in the man's company. The man had a considerable charm, but it was easy and free, rather than something he focused on a person to serve his ends.

"Sir!" A hand was tugging at his stirrup. Ruadhan looked down to see a woman in a blue kirtle jogging next to him. He stopped his horse. "What is it, good lady?" he asked.

"My boy, Stephen. He stepped off the road to attend to... relieving himself," she said, blushing. "He has not returned, and it has been some time."

"How long has he been gone?" asked Ruadhan, frowning.

"Perhaps half of an hour?" the woman guessed.

"Which side of the road?" The woman pointed to the right.

"I'll go look for him," said Ruadhan, gesturing to his

sergeants to continue their shepherding of the rest of the pilgrims.

The Irish knight surveyed the landscape as he pushed his horse to a light canter. This section of the road was fairly barren, and if the boy was embarrassed to relieve himself in front of others, he would have had a bit of a job finding some concealing cover. The only thing close enough was a small rocky promontory in the middle distance. Ruadhan cursed softly under his breath and increased the pace of his horse.

"Hallo?" he called out as he approached the outcropping. No sense in terrifying anyone.

There was no answer.

Cautious, Ruadhan veered wide and rounded the side of the promontory from a distance, his shield up.

The first arrow struck his shield with a heavy thud, and he almost dropped it. The second hissed through the air and bit into the shoulder of his horse. Behind the outcropping, at least twenty men lay in concealment. Others were hidden amidst the rocks and had obviously been watching his approach the entire time.

Ruadhan's horse reared, and for a brief moment, all of his energy was occupied with keeping his seat. The stallion was terrified and angry but had been well trained; he was able to channel the steed's energies into turning and galloping away at full speed.

Another arrow hissed by his head as Ruadhan bent low over the saddle. He gripped the reins with one hand and pulled his horn from a saddle bag as he raced across the flat terrain. Pursing his lips, he sounded the horn, blowing a warning blast to his fellow knights. He was preparing to sound the horn again when two arrows sank into his horse's rump, and the poor beast abruptly sat down on its hind legs with a scream.

Ruadhan threw himself from the wounded horse, getting his legs clear before the animal rolled on them and trapped him. He pushed himself to his feet and drew his sword, crouching low behind his shield. The bandits had abandoned their hiding place and were streaming out on either side of the rocks. Some of them were on horseback. On foot and in chain mail, there was no way that Ruadhan would be able to make it back to the pilgrim caravan. He tightened his grip on his sword and his shield. He would make his stand here.

The bandits on horseback were archers with short recurve bows designed for speed rather than power. Ruadhan doubted that their arrows could penetrate his mail, but his head was vulnerable, and he did not have the time to drop his weapon and pull on the hood of his chain mail. None of the bandits seemed anything more than lightly armed and armoured. Ruadhan would certainly be able to buy the rest of his group at least a little time. If only he wasn't completely on his own, with nothing to guard his back, that is. Once the bandits got round him, they would finish him quickly.

So Ruadhan prepared to die, planning to take as many of his enemies with him as he could manage. "Non nobis domine, non nobis," he murmured, "sed nomine tuo da gloriam."

*Not to us Lord, not to us, but to Your name, give the glory.*

His horse was no longer struggling. Ruadhan backed towards it so that he could at least have some cover behind him. Thank goodness the horse archers were staying back, providing covering fire for the bandits charging on foot. He tried to estimate their numbers, and reckoned there were perhaps fifteen of them.

Suddenly, Ruadhan could hear the sound of hoofbeats approaching from behind. *Had one of them got behind him? Were there more ambushers?* He didn't want to turn away from the attackers in front, but he didn't want to be struck from behind, either.

"Friend to your rear! Friend to your rear!" came the furious shout, and in the space of a second, a knight on horseback shot past him and charged into the mass of approaching bandits. The knight cut through them like a scythe at harvest time, the bulk of his warhorse knocking men aside even as the warrior brought his sword down amongst them time and again.

It was Oliver Oakeshott. He had not waited to pull on his armour, but had simply charged into the fray, and had thrown the bandit attack into confusion.

*He needs my help!* Ruadhan could not run with great speed in his armour, but he moved toward the combat as best he could, managing a steady jog. He tried to will himself to be faster, but knew that once off his horse, a mailed knight had little speed.

Unarmoured, Oliver had obviously decided that speed was his best ally. He did not allow himself to become entangled with fighting one person in particular but moved from opponent to opponent without pause. The horse archers could not shoot at him without risk of hitting their own fighters.

Slowly, far too slowly, Ruadhan was reaching the knot of fighting men. At least six or seven had fallen, and all of their attention was focused upon the unarmoured knight on horseback. Ruadhan stumbled but managed to catch himself. Running in armour had cost him a great deal of energy.

Nevertheless, Oliver's timely charge had given Ruadhan a chance at life, a chance of surviving this wholly unexpected ambush. The English knight had risked his life to give Ruadhan that chance, and such bravery had to be answered. The Irish knight bellowed as he raised his sword and charged into the knot of men trying to surround Oliver and bring him down.

Ruadhan's charge bought Oliver the chance to break free once again and continue to wreak havoc amongst the bandits. Their swords swept back and forth, heavy blows that crumpled bodies and laid men low. Ruadhan could feel the tide of the fight beginning to turn. The bandits' attacks were already less fierce, and there was greater reluctance among the enemy to engage the knights and risk injury or death.

Finally, as if a string had been suddenly cut, the bandits' nerve abruptly broke, and they began to retreat.

Oliver whooped and prepared to charge at them, but Ruadhan shouted a warning. "No pursuit! No pursuit!" he shouted. "Do you see those horse archers? They will make a hedgehog out of you. Let them go. If we break off, the archers will not fire."

"How do you know?" challenged Oliver, breathing heavily.

"It is how they fight," replied Ruadhan.

"Strange way of fighting."

Ruadhan shrugged. "Even so."

The two knights looked at each other as they fought to regain their breath. Ruadhan leaned on his sword. "Oliver Oakeshott," he said, looking up, "I believe you saved my life."

Oliver reached for his canteen, took a deep drink, and tossed it down to Ruadhan. "Come on," he said, indicating a space behind him, "I'll even give you a ride back to the caravan. Speaking of which, where are the rest of your Templar friends?"

Ruadhan took a drink from Oliver's canteen, shaded his eyes, and peered back to the pilgrim road. There was an enormous cloud of dust. "Hellfire!" he swore. "There must have been other bandits. Come on!" He hauled himself up onto Oliver's stallion, which stepped sideways and whinnied in complaint at the extra weight.

"Merciful mother Mary," said Oliver as he gently steered his horse around, "do you Templars really do this sort of thing all the time?"

---

There had indeed been other bandits on the other side of the pilgrim road; the pair discovered that another ambush had been launched when Ruadhan had sounded his horn in warning, but it had failed. "They panicked, if I'm any judge of these things," said Hugh Thomas as the Templar brothers gathered. "They meant to hit us on both flanks, but you threw off their timing. We didn't chase them far, mind. Those damnable horse archers."

"Any losses?" asked Ruadhan, looking at their numbers.

"Just your horse," said Gautier de Mesnil, with a hint of a sneer. "You can borrow one of mine for the rest of the journey. Oh, and a few of the peasants, who couldn't run quickly enough."

"I have a spare mount. Thank you, brother," replied Ruadhan evenly. Suddenly, he remembered the reason he had been riding away from the road. "Damnation. There's still a missing boy. I was looking for him when this all started." He turned and strode towards his sergeants, calling for a horse.

"Don't go alone!" Hugh called after him. "Take that English knight with you. He seems handy enough."

Ruadhan and Oliver rode past the scene of their brief battle, where carrion birds were already beginning their work upon the bodies of the fallen. Oliver glanced down curiously. "So those must be Saracens," he said. "I've always wondered what they'd look like."

"They're not all the same," said Ruadhan as they continued towards the rocky outcropping. "Some are Turks, some are Egyptians, some are Syrians, some are Nizaris...and that's not even counting the ones who look Saracen but are Christian: Armenians, Jacobites, and so on. And then there's the Jews, of course."

"It all sounds very complicated. Is there a guidebook or something?"

"You can read?" asked Ruadhan in surprise.

"All manner of things were beaten into my head in my youth. Can you?"

"I'm Irish," said Ruadhan. "We were reading and writing before the rise of Rome."

"Never heard that before."

"Of course not. The English are raised to lie about the Irish because they are so jealous of us."

Oliver laughed. "So, there is a sense of humour underneath all that chainmail." Suddenly, he turned somber. "That's our missing boy, I think."

Thrown among the rocks was the body of a young boy, his throat cut.

Ruadhan slipped from his saddle and lifted the child's body. "Come on," he said sadly. "Let's take him back so that his mother can bury him."

As it turned out, however, his mother had also died in the bandit attack. Ruadhan and Oliver buried the boy themselves at the side of the road with the other fallen pilgrims.

Despite the morning's troubles, the caravan managed to reach the village of Ma'arat just as the full heat of the day was rising.

"Thank the heavens!" gasped Hugh Thomas, wiping his sweating face with a cloth freshly cooled by water from the village's well. "Sergeant Fuller, take the men and set up the tents, if you please. We'll be glad of the shade soon enough." His sergeant nodded, and the Templar men at arms began to work at erecting open canvas coverings that would provide shelter from the sun while allowing the air to flow through them.

"Those look like a good idea," said Oliver, taking a long drink of water as he ambled over to the Templars. "Simon, do we have one of those?"

"No, milord."

"That's a shame. Perhaps you should look around the village and see if we can buy one. I'll even let you share it with me."

"Yes, milord."

Oliver turned to the Templars, who were regarding the exchange with some amusement. "And if he's going tent shopping, that means *someone* needs to take care of the horses. I think we can all guess who that will be. Damn and blast, but I could use some more servants." With a wave, the English knight stomped off.

"What an extraordinary fellow," said Hugh Thomas in astonishment. He turned to Ruadhan. "How was he against the bandits? We didn't even know what was happening at first; just saw him take off hell for leather, as if the devil himself was after him. A moment later, and we had our own problems, of course."

"That reminds me," said Ruadhan, "why did you not send

my sergeants to me after I sounded the horn? I could have used them."

"I commandeered them," said Gautier casually. "We were facing the larger force, and with that English fellow haring after you, I was sure you had things well in hand."

Hugh and Bernard looked troubled at this but remained silent.

Ruadhan knew better than to challenge Gautier on the point, which would accomplish nothing other than giving secret enjoyment to the French Templar. "In answer to your question," he said, turning slightly away from Gautier and towards the others, "he fought like a lion. There were perhaps fifteen or twenty bandits who attacked. Less than five survived to run away, and those would not have escaped without archer cover."

"An enemy force can look very large through frightened eyes," drawled Gautier. The other Templars flushed, but Ruadhan simply smiled.

"Ah! That explains why you commandeered my men," he said to the Frenchman.

Hugh tried to cover his laugh with a cough. Gautier's eyes flashed angrily, and the man turned on his heel and stalked away.

Bernard shook his head. "I do not think he is a good man to have as an enemy."

Ruadhan snorted. "The choice was his, not mine."

---

There was little in the way of a breeze that afternoon in the village of Ma'arat, and the heat was stifling. Ruadhan knew that he should eat but had no appetite, so he chewed on a few salted olives and left it at that. Oliver's man Simon had managed to find an open-faced tent for purchase, but instead of being made of durable canvas, it was cloth dyed a ridiculous-looking purple. Oliver seemed entirely untroubled by the people staring and chuckling at his garish shelter, lounging against his bed roll and sharing some wine with his servant.

"Had I not seen him take Gerald de Lanier apart with my own eyes, I would think him a clown," murmured Hugh Thomas, sitting in the shade beside Ruadhan.

"Do you know anything about him?" asked the Irish knight. "I mean, why is he here? He's no pilgrim."

"You've talked to him more than I have," said Hugh. "I asked around after the trial, but everyone I talked to seemed to be just as astonished as I was. A few of the sergeants had seen him drinking and dicing in the Venetian quarter, but they were very short on details."

"Probably because they had been drinking and dicing in the Venetian quarter," observed Ruadhan.

"Not my business what the sergeants get up to in their own time. It's not like they've said the vows as we have," said Hugh.

Ruadhan stared at the patterns made by shadows against the roof of the tent. "Do you ever regret the vows you took?" he asked, suddenly curious.

Hugh looked at him in surprise for a moment, then settled back down onto his bed roll. "The vow of poverty? Not really. The Order provides for us well enough, and half of the family sheepfold went to the Order when my father died anyway. The vow of chastity? Well...you know what it's like. Sometimes the urge comes, but it passes. Most of the time," said Hugh with a laugh. "The vow of obedience? That can be a tricky one. I grew up with no masters, save my father and my prince, and no counsel but my own to keep in matters of honour. To be told what to do by a knight ten years my senior, fair enough. But can you imagine if someone like Gautier was selected as Knight Commander or even the Grand Master? I would find it hard to obey that man, and yet I have sworn to obey my superiors in the Order."

"Gautier de Mesnil as Grand Master of the Templars?" Ruadhan laughed as he stared at the roof of the tent. "I'd only have one choice."

"What's that?"

"Go to Damascus and join the Saracens."

---

As the high heat of the afternoon began to fade, the pilgrims of the caravan began to pack up their belongings and form a rough marching order. Ruadhan rode up and down the line, checking on the status of those who carried injuries from the attack earlier in the day. "Remember!" he called out as he rode. "Fill up your jugs and waterskins! We will not have access to water again until morning. This is the last water available for many miles!" He then checked to make sure that his sergeants were also listening, demanding that they show him their canteens. One of them, a man at arms named Edward, paled as he lifted his canteen, realizing that it was empty. The man looked at it more closely and cursed.

"Sorry, Brother. The canteen was pierced by an arrow during the ambush, and I did not notice," the man said, chastened.

"What have you been drinking from the last two hours?" demanded Ruadhan. Edward looked down and did not answer.

"Show me, you fool." The man at arms reached into his saddlebags and pulled out a wineskin. Ruadhan took it and weighed it in his hands. It was at least half full. He shoved it back into the man's hands. "Empty it. Pour it out right now," he said.

The man gaped at him, then pulled the cork at the top and poured out the wine onto the dusty ground. The rest of Ruadhan's sergeants watched silently.

"Now go to the well and fill that skin with water. Then give thanks to God that I found you out. You'd have died of thirst on the road to Jerusalem."

"Yes, Brother. Thank you, Brother," said Edward, and hurried on his way.

"Will you report the man at the next Chapter?" asked Hugh. "A striped back would serve to remind him and would teach the others a lesson as well."

Ruadhan shook his head. "I find the lash to be a hard teacher, and not a very good one at that. I do not like to treat men as worse than dogs."

"You're a strange fellow, Ruadhan," said Hugh. "That English knight is not the only odd one on this journey."

"No, I suppose he is not."

## Chapter Three
### OLIVER

The steady march of the caravan continued as the sun sank lower and lower on the horizon, and the shadows of dusk began to darken the landscape. "Damned strange way to travel," said Oliver. "Do you think they mean to keep travelling in the darkness?"

"It is the manner of travel in these parts, milord. No one travels in the high heat of the day if it can be helped."

"I don't blame them. Can you imagine wearing full armor like the Templar knights? You could cook an egg on their chain mail. Well, actually, it would run through the links and create an unholy, smelly mess, but you know what I mean."

"Yes, milord."

"Simon, what do you know about the Templars?" asked Oliver. "I must confess I paid them little attention in Acre save to steer clear of them. Knights who are monks? Monks who are knights? Seems like neither fish nor fowl."

"Little enough, milord. They take the three vows, just as the monastic orders do, yet they fight as belted knights," replied Simon.

"Three vows?" echoed Oliver. "You mean poverty, chastity, and obedience?"

"Just so, milord."

"Bless me," said Oliver, "I'm terrible at all three of those things."

Simon kept silent.

Oliver wondered what would make a man choose to restrict his life in such ways. He could understand picking up a sword to escape poverty or agreeing to enter a monastery in exchange for a roof over the head and food on the table, but if God and fortune had provided you with life's necessities and the means to keep them, what red-blooded man would choose to impose such limits on his own living?

"There's a lot that I don't understand about the world, Simon," he concluded aloud.

His servant accepted this pronouncement in silence.

Oliver glanced over at him. "You all right, Simon?" he asked. "You're awfully quiet."

"I do not wish to step into over-familiarity, milord," the man replied.

"God's wounds, Simon, I think we're well past that now. You know practically everything about me – why I had to leave England, the company I keep, all my sinful ways. I should think you're probably the person most familiar with me in the entire world," said Oliver.

"Perhaps, milord, but it is not my place to judge what you do or how you do it."

"Hah! No, that appears to be my father's job," said Oliver with a hint of bitterness. "I mean, they call this land 'Outremer'—literally, 'beyond the sea.' You'd think that would be far enough to escape my father's reach, but you'd be wrong.

Anyway," he said, returning to the gist of their conversation, "what is it you're trying not to be over-familiar about?"

"It is not my place to say, milord," replied Simon stubbornly.

"Oh, have it your way! You're like that story in the Bible. You know, the one about the stubborn donkey?"

"Balaam's ass, milord."

"Exactly! I'm afraid you're being a bit of a Balaam's ass, Simon," said Oliver.

Simon gave an odd little half-smile and said nothing.

---

Eventually, twilight darkened into dusk, and the caravan was obliged to light its way as the pilgrims and their escort proceeded. The night was quiet, save for the sounds of the marching travelers, and even their talk was quiet and subdued. Oliver stifled a yawn as he lifted his torch to check the road ahead. It had been a long day.

He hadn't minded the fight with the bandits; truth be told, it was when he was fighting that he felt the most alive. The world seemed filled with dishonesty and stupidity and often was just dreadfully boring, but combat, well. Combat stripped everything else away and forced you to focus on the *now*, the immediate, what was right in front of you. It was honest, even if the world was not. There was the risk to life and limb, but that was the point. If there were no stakes, combat would be filled with all the artificial nonsense gripping the rest of the world.

*The Irish Templar, Ruadhan Ui Neill, could feel it too.*

Oliver knew it in his bones; the young English knight had devoted himself so thoroughly to combat that he could see what it revealed about other people. There were the fellows who brayed loudly before a fight and tried to make themselves small during it; there were the ones who were terrified but just got on with it as best they could; there were the bullies who scanned the field for those weaker than them, and all manner of variations on these. But there were also the fighters who were meant to be on the field of battle, who could see what would happen next, who moved like wolves amidst the sheep. Oliver was one of those; he had been there for as long as he could remember, and he could tell that Ruadhan was there too.

If Oliver hadn't already been watching the Templar, he might not have noticed so quickly when Ruadhan was in jeopardy from the ambushing bandits. As it was, even as Oliver spurred his horse and raced to join him, he had seen the series of events: sounding the horn to warn the others, racing to escape, losing his horse, turning to fight. It was exactly what Oliver would have done in his place. Ruadhan had quickly accepted the likelihood of his own death and decided to go down fighting. Then, when given a lifeline by Oliver's unexpected charge, the Irishman had seized it with both hands and fought like a lion.

If Oliver was to wager, he would bet that he was a better fighter than Ruadhan. But not by much.

*Do they all fight like that?* If so, the Templars would make a formidable force. Oliver wanted to see more. Wanted to see if there was anyone better at fighting than he was. *I may have to stick close to these Poor Knights of Christ for a while.* He shuddered. *Not to take their vows, though.* Oliver found it hard to imagine a worse fate.

He was broken from his reverie by the sight of torchlight high in the sky ahead of the caravan. A tower?

"Chastel Rouge, milord," offered Simon. "The Red Tower of the Templars."

"Does that mean we can stop wandering in the darkness?" asked Oliver querulously.

"This is our camp until just before dawn, milord."

"God be praised. It seems a bit of a dump, this Red Tower," said Oliver, peering, "unless I'm missing something. It's not actually red, is it?"

"My understanding, milord, is that the tower gets its name from the colour of the nearby stone," replied Simon.

"You really are as good as a travel guide. Dear fellow, I shall see to the horses. That tent looks like a dangerous puzzle and not one I wish to solve." Oliver yawned, dismounted, and stretched. "Did you know my grandfather was in harness until he was past seventy? I don't know how the man did it. A day's ride, and I feel like my ass is going to fall off."

Sometime later, Oliver returned from where the horses were picketed and was delighted to discover that Simon had not only raised the tent but also started a fire and had a stewpot burbling away, hanging from a tripod above the fire.

"I take back every unkind thought I've ever had about you, Simon," said Oliver as he sat down. He glanced over at the squat stone tower a hundred yards or more away. "Not terribly welcoming, these Templars," he observed. "They could at least let us into the courtyard."

"It is their practice, milord, to never open their gates after sundown."

"What, not even to their own Brothers?" asked Oliver in surprise.

"The discipline of the Order is a byword, milord."

"Let's hope those bandits have been thoroughly scared off. How many knights do you think that place holds?"

"I do not know, milord."

"And I thought your knowledge of the Order had no bottom," said Oliver, grinning. "That smells delicious, by the way. Do I want to know what's in it?"

"All manner of healthy things, milord."

"That's what I was afraid of," sighed Oliver.

---

Oliver frowned as he turned and twisted. Sleep was proving to be elusive, and he could not understand why. Simon's stew had been as good as it smelled, the day had been long, and although the night had turned chill, he had a warm blanket. Although he had joked about his sore body, Oliver was used to campaigning and considered his travel conditions to be better than most.

Still, his mind was in full motion, and sleep would not come. His thoughts kept on returning to the skirmish with the bandits.

*Why?* It wasn't the killing; Oliver had slept like a baby after killing Gerald de Lanier in single combat, nor had any of the deaths by his hand ever given him trouble.

*Was it the death of the boy?*

That had been sad, but not a thing that would normally cost him a night's sleep.

*Being attacked so close to Acre?*

That had troubled him as they marched; the bandits had shown unusual daring to attempt an ambush so close to a major city. Still, perhaps they had become exceptionally bold or were extremely desperate.

The more he thought, the more Oliver understood why his mind was racing and how focused he was on the fight.

*Ruadhan Ui Neill.*

The Irishman had looked like some kind of pagan war god

as he stood facing the bandits, determined to die hard. The way that he moved as he fought was graceful and long-limbed. Oliver fought with a kind of stripped-down, brutal efficiency, but Ruadhan moved like water, all sweeps and turns, a distant look in his startling blue eyes as if the man was leading a dance to which only he knew the tune.

Ruadhan's face just after the fight, when he had drunk from the canteen Oliver had passed him, was etched in Oliver's memory. The man's lips had looked so soft as he brought the canteen to his mouth, and when Ruadhan closed his eyes as he drank, his black curls plastered to his face, he had looked like one of the angels whose faces Oliver had so lovingly traced in the family Bible.

*Damn and blast. Damn and blast!*

A long time ago, Oliver had stopped trying to deny the path down which his desires took him. He knew that he wanted and loved in ways that were different from those around him, and that his desires made other people afraid and repelled. However, he had also learned early on that he was not alone in his desires, and that with care and discretion, it was possible to find some fleeting sense of fulfillment in a dangerous world.

But this...this attraction to Ruadhan Ui Neill felt perilous.

*There is a deeper danger here.*

Many, many times, Oliver had looked at different men and felt attraction, desire, a quickening of excitement and lust that had more often than not culminated in a lovely night's distractions. That was not what he was feeling now. Yes, there was that same stirring in his body, and there was no denying the desire, but this felt somehow more cautious, almost like there was a sense of shyness.

Oliver snorted. He'd never felt shy about anything in his

life. And yet, here he was, hesitating over what to do next because he didn't want to put a foot wrong and suddenly have possibilities disappear.

"Sod it," he muttered to himself and threw back the blanket to get up, walk to the well, and get himself some fresh water.

Thankfully, several campfires were still burning low but still providing enough illumination so that he didn't step on a pilgrim. Oliver threaded his way through the encampment, trying to remember where the damnable well was—on the outskirts of the camp, to the north, if he remembered it correctly. As he made his way, the tents and shelters grew sparser, and he chuckled as he heard sounds coming from one tent that were distinctly un-pilgrimish .

Finally, he saw the slight depression in which the well rested. As quietly as he could, he lowered the bucket into the water, let it fill, and drew it up. There was a noise behind him, and Oliver smiled to himself as he turned.

"I wondered if you" – he began, then stopped.

"Wondered what?" asked Gautier de Mesnil, out of armour and dressed in a linen habit. "Tell me, what exactly were you wondering, Oliver Oakeshott?" He stepped close to Oliver, took the bucket of water from his hands, and drank deeply.

Oliver recovered his composure quickly. "I wondered if you were trying to kill your brother knight this afternoon, leaving him alone to fight twenty bandits," he said.

In the darkness, Gautier's eyes glittered with malice. "That was not what you were wondering, Englishman," he said with confidence. "You were hoping you might encounter that same knight you mentioned and find him grateful for saving his life. And how might he express that gratitude?" Gautier's voice was honey.

"Tread carefully, master Templar," breathed Oliver. "Tread very carefully indeed." Though Gautier was standing far too close, he did not step back one inch.

"Indeed, I should be careful with a man who is so dangerous in single combat," said Gautier. "I watched you kill Gerald de Lanier, sir knight. Very dangerous indeed. I," drawled the Frenchman, placing a hand on Oliver's chest, "would be helpless against such a fierce warrior. He could do whatever he wanted with me."

Oliver's eyes widened as he took in Gautier's meaning. "You have come to the wrong place for what you seek," he said firmly, moving the Templar's hand from his chest.

"Have I?" whispered Gautier. "I have seen the way you watch the Irishman. What does that ignorant bogtrotter possess that I do not? Cast your eyes away from dross and feast them on French gold." He snaked an arm around Oliver's neck and sought to bring him closer.

Oliver pulled back against the French knight's surprisingly strong grip. "As I said, sir, you are mistaken," he said. "Please take your company elsewhere." He pushed the Templar back.

Gautier's glittering eyes became guarded. "Mistaken? How so? I but desired a drink of water. Good night, Sir Oliver," he said, backing away. "Let us hope we do not need more of your martial prowess tomorrow." He turned and slipped away into the night.

It was a long time before Oliver was finally able to find sleep that night.

Oliver felt as though he had only just closed his eyes when Simon was shaking him to wake once more. "For the sake of the Blessed Virgin, man, it's still dark out! Can't you wake me at a time that makes sense?"

"I am sorry, milord. The caravan will be on its way before dawn."

Forgoing any further commentary, Oliver shoved his blanket away and stood up, shuffling around to shake the stiffness out of his muscles and joints. It had gotten surprisingly cold in the night.

"Never mind the horses, Simon; I'll take care of them. You pack up this travelling carnival you call a tent," he said.

"Yes, milord."

As Oliver stomped towards the picket lines of the horses, he was caught by an astonishing scent; a rich, earthy aroma that seemed to be emanating from the tents where the Templar brothers had spent the night.

He hesitated a moment. He really did not want to see Gautier, with his sly insinuations. Still, Oliver was damned if he would curtail his own movements because of someone else's oily ways. So, with rather more force than he intended to, he strode into the Templar section of camp, where the brother knights seated around a fire looked up at him in surprise.

"Forgive me, noble sirs," Oliver said, collecting himself with a sheepish grin, "I caught a scent of heaven and followed it here."

The knights looked at each other and laughed. Oliver was relieved to note that Gautier was nowhere to be seen. "I've never heard of a nose leading anyone to heaven," said Bernard, "but what brought you here is something called *qahwa*, in the

Saracen tongue. Boiling water poured over a kind of roasted ground-up bean."

"We like ours with a hint of sugar in it," added Ruadhan, handing Oliver a metal cup filled with a dark brown liquid. "Try some. Be careful, it's hot."

Oliver sipped cautiously at it. He closed his eyes and made a sound of deep contentment. "Gracious Saviour, no wonder you're able to get up and start your day so early," he said in wonderment. "I could become very used to this! A Saracen drink, you say?"

"As far as we can tell," said Hugh. "Although the Romans drank it, apparently. They called it *arabicum*."

"I call it morning salvation," said Oliver reverently. He looked around the encampment. "You seem to be short one Templar," he said casually.

"Haven't seen him since last night," said Bernard. "He does this on the road sometimes. He'll be here when it is time to leave."

"And everything has been packed and made ready," added Hugh pointedly. The others chuckled.

Oliver stood up. "Brothers, I take my leave of you," he said, "but thank you for the gift of *qahwa*." He stumbled over the word. "There must be an easier name for it. At any rate, thank you once again, and I will see you on the road."

By the time he reached the horses, Simon had already fed them and rubbed them down.

"My beloved servant, you must forgive me," said Oliver, handing Simon the metal cup and beginning to sort out tack and harness. "I was distracted by my quest for a heavenly elixir and have not performed my horsely duties. Have yourself a sip of that. Careful, it's still hot."

He lifted a saddle on and began to cinch the girth as his servant took a drink from the cup. Simon's eyes widened. "My goodness, milord," he said, a tone of wonder in his voice, "I have never tasted such a thing."

"I know, dear fellow, I know! The Saracens call it *qahwa*, apparently. Do see if you can find some at the next village we stop at, there's a good man."

Whatever Simon's response might have been was interrupted by a stirring within the camp. There were shouts and a woman's scream. At first Oliver thought it must be another attack and quickly mounted his horse, but then he furrowed his brow. "This does not have the sound of combat," he said to Simon, who was holding the reins of his own horse. "Go on and find out what's going on."

A few moments later, Simon returned, looking disturbed. "There has been a murder in the night, milord."

## Chapter Four
### RUADHAN

He looked down at the body of a man who had been, if Ruadhan was any judge, in his early thirties. The dead man's throat looked like a single livid bruise, and the man's tongue hung obscenely out of the side of his mouth.

"Has anyone claimed to know the man?" asked Ruadhan, turning to the priest who had summoned the Templar knights to see the body.

"Not well, Brother," the priest replied. "Some folk who said that they talked to him yesterday as they walked the road. His name was Arnaldo, an artisan from Venice. Kept to himself, aside from some little chat with his fellow pilgrims."

"With whom did he chat?" asked Bernard. "Can you bring them to us, please?"

The priest went off on his errand, and the Templars stepped closer to confer. "You know we have no writ of law here," said Hugh.

"Agreed," said Bernard, "but at least we can make a report to the royal court when we arrive in Jerusalem. We will carry out no justice, but we can investigate and relay our findings."

"Brothers! What tragedy has happened here?" asked Gautier de Mesnil as he caught up with the others.

"Where have you been, then?" demanded Hugh Thomas. Ruadhan silently examined the figure of Gautier. He wasn't interested in the man's story, certain that it would be a lie. Instead, he regarded the tale that the man's appearance told – carefully dressed, clean face, hair brushed and parted.

"Why were you in the Red Tower last night?" Ruadhan asked him.

Surprise passed across Gautier's face, followed by irritation.
*Ah. A guess, but a correct one.*

"Brother Emil, the commander of the Tower, wanted to hear firsthand about the ambush yesterday, so he sent for one of us. I was nearest, so I went. It was late by the time I finished, so I passed the night there."

"We must tell Emil what has transpired in the night," said Bernard, turning to the others. "This is within his writ of law; the murder happened on Templar land."

"The killing may have happened on Templar territory," objected Hugh, "but unless a Templar is involved, Emil has no authority here."

"Perhaps," said Ruadhan in a wry voice, "we should try to determine what happened first, and the rest can follow."

By this time, the priest had returned with a pilgrim in tow. He stared down at the body of the murdered man. "This is the one who talked with Arnaldo yesterday," the priest announced. "Peter, tell these worthy Brothers who you are," he added, giving the man a prod.

"My name is Peter, worthy sirs," said the man, clutching a

cloth cap in his hands, "they sometimes call me Peter Thistle. This is my second pilgrimage to Jerusalem, lords," he added.

"How did you know the murdered man, Peter Thistle?" asked Ruadhan.

"Not well, my lords, not well," replied Peter, running a hand through his hair. "I met him on the road yesterday for the first time. Neither of us had a horse, you see, and so we fell into pace with those who were walking the road. Sometimes you get to talking, to pass the time, and so it was with Arnaldo and a few others."

"What did you talk about?" asked Bernard.

"This and that, sirs, this and that," replied Peter. "Nothing of any great importance. I told him of my trade as a cooper. He told me of his trade as a silversmith. Beautiful work he did, too."

Ruadhan frowned. "How do you know that he did beautiful work?"

"I saw the man's work, lords!" said Peter. "It was hanging from his neck and slipped out when he tripped upon a stone. He had made a beautiful silver pendant that he was giving as a gift to the Canons when we reached the Holy Sepulchre in Jerusalem. Gorgeous thing. An apple, lords, such as from the story of the Garden of Eden."

*An odd choice to give as a gift to the keepers of the tomb of the Lord.*

Ruadhan's frown deepened.

"Father," asked Hugh, "did you find this pendant upon the man's body?"

"No, Brother," replied the priest, "but I will search for it when I prepare the body for burial."

"Thank you, Father," said Hugh. " Please make a list of his things. If this pendant appears, we will want to see it."

"Is there anything else you can tell us, Peter Thistle?" asked Bernard. "Was there anything else that you learned about the man?"

"Only that he was from Venice, lords, and that this was his first time in the kingdom," said Peter.

"You may go," said Hugh. "Thank you, Master Thistle."

"Wait," said Ruadhan sharply. The others turned to look at him, and Peter paused, his face expressing uncertainty. "You said that you chatted on the road with Arnaldo and a few others. Who are these others that you mentioned, and why have they not come forward?"

Peter shook his head sadly. "Because they cannot come forward, my lord. The others we chatted with were Matilde and her boy, Philippe. He was the boy that went missing yesterday, and she was killed in the ambush by those accursed bandits."

---

Ruadhan ignored the other Templars as they argued fiercely among themselves. He tried to focus his thoughts. Surely, these events could not be coincidental; they had to be connected, but how?

*Gautier. That slimy piece of wolf shit. I don't know how he's mixed up in this, but I can feel his touch.*

Even as Ruadhan was thinking this, Gautier spoke to the gathering, low and urgent. "You should know, Brothers, that I saw the English knight wandering the campsite after dark. I was answering Brother Emil's summons and saw him moving through the camp long after everyone had gone to sleep."

"The English knight, you say?" Hugh's voice was doubtful. "Sir Oliver?"

"The very same," murmured Gautier. "I did not ask him his business, as I was busy with my own errand."

Ruadhan felt a stone settle in his belly. In truth, he barely knew the Englishman, but he had fought beside him the previous day, and felt he had the measure of the man. "We saw Sir Oliver fight the bandits toe to toe," Ruadhan observed, "hardly the behaviour of a man who kills in the night like a coward."

"And yet, what do we really know about him?" insisted Gautier. "When he went before the court this past week, it was for attacking a Venetian citizen."

"God found him innocent in the trial by combat," Bernard reminded them.

"So He did, Brother, so He did," replied Gautier and let the silence hang uncomfortably.

"This gets us nowhere," said Hugh. "Brother Gautier, go inform Brother Emil of what has happened. Templar law may not hold here, but this is Templar land. He should be made aware. Brother Bernard, make arrangements with the priest for the burial. We must not delay too long. We still have more than a hundred pilgrim souls in our care and have lost our morning start. Brother Ruadhan, go and have speech with Sir Oliver as we travel. See if you can gain some measure of the man's character."

"Perhaps Brother Ruadhan and I should trade our tasks?" inquired Gautier. "The man did save Brother Ruadhan's life yesterday. Some might say that would lead to a less than impartial judgement."

Ruadhan flushed and made to speak, but Hugh was faster. "Sir Oliver is not on trial, and Brother Ruadhan is not his judge," he said, irritation colouring his tone. "I hold the watch for this caravan and will answer for any decisions I make before the Chapter when our duty is done."

"Of course, Brother," said Gautier, his eyes hooded. "I did not mean to imply otherwise."

---

The burial was quick and with minimal ceremony; the Knight Commander of the Red Tower, Brother Emil, promised that the grave would shortly have a proper headstone and that a message would be sent to the Venetian Quarter of Acre to inform them of the death of one of their citizens. The caravan resumed their journey shortly thereafter, and Ruadhan made his way to ride beside Oliver.

*I feel like a fool. This man is a killer, yes, but not a murderer. I know that there is a difference.*

"A sorry business," said Ruadhan as he caught up alongside the Englishman and his servant.

"A lot of death for one day, absent a battlefield," replied Oliver. "Missing children, ambushes, and a murder to crown it. A Holy Kingdom, indeed."

"What do you mean by that? Do you not think the Kingdom of Jerusalem a holy place?" asked Ruadhan.

Oliver chuckled. "Forgive me if I spoke too freely," he said. "Simon constantly tells me to hold my tongue. Well, he doesn't say it, of course, but he gets silent in a very pointed way. No, I do not mean to insult the kingdom. I just haven't seen anything in my time here to distinguish this place from any other I have been. I don't know whether that makes all places holy, or none at all."

Ruadhan paused. Although he liked Oliver's easy and carefree manner, this verged on mockery.

"I promised my life to defend God's kingdom," he said softly, and wondered at his own hypocrisy.

*You had your reasons for joining the Order, and you know it. Who are you to sit upon a high horse and look down?*

Oliver glanced at him. "I have offended you! Forgive me. I should listen more carefully to Simon's silences. I did not mean to cast aspersions upon your choice. Every man must have a master, and if he is lucky, he gets to choose. How can anyone be faulted for choosing God as their master?"

"And you?" asked Ruadhan. "Whom have you chosen as your master?"

"I am young, Brother Ruadhan," Oliver replied, laughing. "I am still weighing my options."

Ruadhan cursed at himself. This was not how he had intended the conversation to go. Instead of drawing the man out, he had gotten his own back up and was being stiff and awkward. He had no idea of how to proceed and felt like a fool.

"So, what made you choose your master, Brother Ruadhan? You are perhaps only a little older than me and far from home. You've picked a hard path. Why?" asked Oliver.

Ruadhan came within a hair's breadth of telling Oliver the whole truth and was shocked at himself. He'd never told anyone; why tell a man he barely knew on the road to Jerusalem? He realized that deep inside himself, he did not want to lie to this man. However, telling him the truth was not even to be considered.

*But I will not lie.*

"It's...complicated," he finally managed, wincing at his clumsiness.

Oliver eyed him. "I see," he replied. "Well, we have a journey ahead of us; if you choose to share this complexity, I would be interested to hear about it. If not, I won't judge. Every man deserves his secrets."

Ruadhan had never wanted to share his confidences more in his entire life. His throat hurt, as if the words were trying to force their way out physically.

"Perhaps," he managed.

Oliver leaned over in his saddle and clapped Ruadhan on the shoulder. "Good God, man, it seems I tread from swamp to quicksand! I dare not even look at Simon; I can feel his silence from here. Shall we discuss the weather? I'll start. It seems very hot today, just like every other day since I arrived here."

Despite himself, Ruadhan smiled. "And yet, some days there is rain. Have you not seen it?"

"Is there really? I must have slept through those days. I suppose there would have to be rain; things do grow in this kingdom, do they not?"

"Oliver, have you ever left Acre?" asked Ruadhan.

"Why would I?" responded Oliver, his hands wide.

Ruadhan stared at him in astonishment. "To see the river where Saint John baptized our Lord? The mountain from which Jesus ascended into Heaven? The tomb in which He broke the power of death for all time? To touch a piece of the very cross upon which He sacrificed Himself to save our souls?"

Oliver eyed him doubtfully. "Well, I do enjoy a nice view from the top of a mountain," he ventured.

Ruadhan was thunderstruck. "You're serious." He gestured toward the horizon. "The Sermon on the Mount – where our Lord performed the miracle of the loaves and fishes – a week's journey away! We could stop off in Cana, where He turned water into wine! Every inch of this land speaks of the deeds of God!"

"Where you supposed to piss, then?" challenged Oliver.

"What?"

"First thing I did this morning after I woke up was go for a piss. Did I accidentally piss on the burial site of Queen Bathsheba? Last night, did I shit where Jacob wrestled with an angel? People have to live here, Ruadhan. This Holy Land you're talking about? There's no room for people!" insisted Oliver.

Unable to fathom what Oliver was saying, Ruadhan felt himself become cold and distant. "I must patrol this flank of the caravan," he said and rode off.

---

It took quite some time for Ruadhan to calm his mind. He realized that all of Oliver's words would be much easier to deal with if he could simply dismiss the man as a fool and, therefore, his words as the utterings of an ignorant lout or, worse, a heretic.

But he did not think Oliver was a fool. Truth be told, he was drawn to the English knight in a way he had never felt before. Ruadhan did not want to think poorly of the man. He liked his company, enjoyed his conversation, was in awe of his fighting ability, and just...wanted to be with him.

Which was why Oliver's words had hurt. Ruadhan had heard cynical commentary on holiness and hypocrisy before—jokes about lustful monks and foolish virgins were commonplace—but something about Oliver's words had cut him deeply.

*Was it what was said, or who was saying it?*

Ruadhan wasn't sure. He liked and admired Oliver, and for

the English knight to aim at the kingdom's holy nature was painful to hear. He did not know if an admiration and affection for Oliver could cohabitate with his love for this storied land where God had wrought His greatest miracles.

Later, when he went to relieve himself, he swore at Oliver, unable to forget the knight's observations and wondering if he had pissed on anything important.

## Chapter Five
### OLIVER

"Simon?" asked Oliver after a long journey in silence, the heat of the day a constant oppressive weight.

"Milord?"

"Am I wrong about everything, Simon?"

"That is a rather broad question, milord."

"For a moment, just for a moment, I was able to look around this land and see it as that damned Templar sees it," said Oliver irritably. "It was a place of wonders, Simon! Rich in history, a land of fables, myths, and stories from the Bible. A place where miracles can happen. A place that's magic."

"Yes, milord."

"But as soon as I think that, what comes into my head? Dicing, less than a week ago. That bloody ship's captain, dandling that young girl on his knee, fumbling up her dress to play with her cunt while he gambled. No lightning struck him down, no boils erupted over his body. How can that *be*, Simon? How can this place be sacred in the eyes of God and yet also a refuge for the criminal and perverse?"

"It is said that God works in mysterious ways, milord," replied Simon.

"Bah! That's no answer at all!" cried Oliver in frustration. "That's what everyone says and acts like it means something, when all it means is that we're not supposed to question anything! A child is saved; it's God's will. A child drowns; it's God's will. And we just accept them both. Why is one a miracle and the other not, if both happened at God's command?"

"Perhaps you have forgotten that Satan also works his evil in the world, milord."

"Huh. That fellow. Don't even get me started on that fellow, Simon. Why is it that you always seem to have an answer to these deep questions?"

"Perhaps it is God's will, milord," replied his servant.

"Look at me, Simon," Oliver commanded and stopped his horse. He glared at his servant's upturned face, which did not show a hint of a smile. "Hmph. I have lost count of the sheer number of times I suspect you are winding me up. One of these times, I will catch you laughing behind my back, Simon, and there will be a reckoning." He twitched the reins to get his horse moving again.

"As you say, milord," replied Simon.

"But that day is not today."

"No, milord."

"Mind you, the day is yet young," said Oliver darkly.

"Yes, milord."

---

By afternoon, the caravan was sheltering in a small village along the road from Acre to Jerusalem. The village featured not only a well but also a small oasis, and some trees provided shade. The villagers offered figs and honeyed sweets for sale, but the heat had driven away Oliver's appetite. He had a terrible headache and suspected that he had not been as careful with water as he should have been, which only added to his foul mood.

Throughout the morning, he had been thinking about how Ruadhan looked at this kingdom. Seen through the Templar's eyes, this was a place of wonders. Seen through Oliver's eyes, the kingdom was hot, dusty, and reeked of camel shit. For the whole of his youth, Oliver had known that he saw things differently from many others. He had always believed that he possessed a clarity of vision that prevented him from falling into snares that cynical men set for the gullible. For the first time, Oliver wondered if there was something he was missing.

He moodily got up and walked towards the well, throwing a date stone into the dirt. Oliver knew he should try to catch some sleep, but he had a stabbing pain in his head. He hated the combination of sweat and dust that had taken up residence in every crevice of his body, and he was angry at the idea that he might have gotten some important things wrong.

*Damn and blast.* The Templar was at the well, drawing water. Oliver would have turned around, but it would have been too obvious, so he just gave Ruadhan a perfunctory nod and sat on a rock to wait until the Irishman was done.

The silence hung awkwardly between them, and Oliver couldn't help himself.

"Which well is this, then?" he asked.

"What?" asked Ruadhan, turning around.

"Which well? Is this where Joseph's brothers threw him after he got a fancy coat? Or where the Samaritan woman drew water for the Judean woman…or was it the other way around?"

Ruadhan turned back to the task of drawing up the bucket. "This is just an ordinary well. I would thank you not to mock me," he said distantly.

"I'm an idiot," said Oliver. "I thought to lighten the mood between us with a jest. I was wrong."

Ruadhan did not turn back around, but Oliver could tell that he was listening.

"Let me begin again," said Oliver.

Ruadhan let go of the handle, and the bucket fell back down the well, hitting the water with a splash.

"I will come back for water later," he said coldly and marched off.

---

The sun was low in the sky, and the pilgrim caravan was on the march when Oliver tried again. He rode up beside the Templar and said, "I would like to explain something to you, and I hope you will listen."

Ruadhan said nothing, but neither did he speed up nor slow down.

"Ruadhan..." began Oliver, "when I told you that I had never left Acre, you looked at me as if I was some strange creature out of a children's story. I felt stupid, embarrassed. I wanted to hit back, to make you feel like you were a fool for looking at this kingdom with eyes of wonder. I lashed out, and I am sorry for it."

For an uncomfortably long time, Ruadhan did not speak. Finally, he said, "Oliver, my words were laced with anger because I find that your opinion matters to me for whatever reason. To hear you so casually dismiss things that I care about shocked me. I also lashed out, and I, too, am sorry for it."

After a pause, Ruadhan continued. "I have served in the kingdom for over a year and am not a fool. I see many of the same things as you – casual cruelties, sins of the flesh and the spirit. I don't know why God permits such things to happen any more than you do. But I do also feel God's presence here. To look upon the tomb of our Lord? To see the waters He walked over, the coast where he told the Apostles that He would make them fishers of men? It thrills me, Oliver; it thrills me to my bones. I can look down an alley and see the foulness of man, but I can also kneel before the Sepulchre and feel God's grace."

"I think you have something that I have lost," said Oliver quietly. "Perhaps you can help me find it again?"

"You ask for bread; I will not give you a stone," said Ruadhan, smiling.

"That sounds Biblical. The Gospel according to Luke?" asked Oliver, tilting his head.

"Close. Matthew," replied Ruadhan.

"Always get those two confused. I'm more of an Old Testament sort of person, anyway. Eye for an eye and all that."

Ruadhan laughed. "Why doesn't that surprise me?"

Oliver joined him in laughter, then said mischievously, "So, my opinion matters to you?"

Ruadhan raised a warning finger. "Don't go using my own words against me."

"I'm not, honestly!" replied Oliver, lifting his hands. "I'm glad my opinion matters, especially since I've spent the last five minutes explaining that your opinion matters to me. Puts us on a more even footing."

The pair rode along in companionable silence for a while

until Oliver innocently asked, "Are we anywhere near where Lucifer offered to make Jesus the ruler of the world?"

Ruadhan frowned. "I don't think so. Why?"

"I need to piss. That seems like an appropriate spot."

The Templar burst out laughing. "Oliver Oakeshott, you are impossible."

"Don't share your opinion with my servant Simon. He doesn't need anyone else to agree with him. Are you listening, Simon?"

"No, milord."

"Our Lord knows when you're lying, Simon."

"Hush, Oliver!" Ruadhan remonstrated. "We've only just mended fences over your mockery of the Lord. Would you really have us at loggerheads again so soon?"

"But it's true!" protested Oliver. "And Simon needs to know it. Fear of God is the only thing that keeps the man from slitting my throat in the night and fleeing to Baghdad."

"Why Baghdad?"

"Simon's always wanted a flying carpet. Couldn't tell you why, but who understands the hearts of men?" asked Oliver rhetorically.

Once more, Ruadhan's laughter echoed in the evening air. "You're ridiculous."

"Part of my charm."

They spent some time riding in companionable silence until Oliver said, "So there was a murder."

Ruadhan nodded. "A grim business, and as yet unresolved. Someone in this caravan is a murderer. I can't help but feel some strange currents running underneath this death." He told Oliver of the conversation with Peter Thistle and what the Templars had learned.

Oliver whistled low. "That is a number of coincidences. An uncomfortable number."

"I agree!" replied Ruadhan. "You see what I mean. The boy, the woman, and the silversmith. All seen talking to each other, and all three dead. A missing pendant, perhaps. And why an apple? That seems an odd gift to the priests."

Oliver nodded. "I had not considered that. It is a strange choice! I mean, the most famous apple in the Bible..."

"Is the fruit of the tree of the knowledge of good and evil," finished Ruadhan. "Eating it was the original sin, for which Adam and Eve were cast out of paradise. Who would wish for such a symbol?"

Oliver frowned. "Unless it's pagan? You hear stories of the apples of youth in the old Greek tales."

"But again, why would you make that as a gift for good Christian priests?" persisted Ruadhan. "No, there is something to this pendant that is more than I can fathom. Let us simply grant that it is a strange choice for the moment."

"And you are sure it is gone?" asked Oliver.

Ruadhan nodded. "At least we can say that it was not found on Arnaldo's body. As to who took it, and when, we do not know."

A call went up from the front of the caravan. They had reached their destination for their second night of marching; this time, an oasis a few hundred yards from the road.

"I must look after the horses while Simon puts up the tent," said Oliver. "This conversation shall be continued."

Ruadhan nodded and rode off to join his brothers.

For the second night in a row, Oliver had difficulty sleeping. His thoughts were once more a tangled skein, only this time twice as knotted. On the one hand was his conversation with Ruadhan about how to look at the world. There was a great deal to consider there, and all of it was tinged with the uncomfortable feeling that Oliver had made himself far too vulnerable to someone he had just met and barely knew. Those thoughts were painful and raw, and he did not need to work hard at convincing himself to put them aside.

On the other hand was the question of the murdered pilgrim. Ruadhan was right to speak about strange currents. Three people had spoken with the Venetian – the boy, his mother, and this Peter Thistle fellow. Now, the boy and his mother were dead, leaving only the cooper.

Oliver sat up. "Damn and blast," he muttered. He had to find Peter Thistle. There was a strong chance the man would not live to see the morning. Oliver pushed his blanket away and stood up, looking around the encampment. He didn't even know what Peter Thistle looked like, let alone where the man was camped.

His frustration was coupled with a rising sense of urgency.
*What to do?*
*Ruadhan.*
At the very least, the Templar had seen the cooper and might have some idea of where the man could be found.

Quietly, Oliver approached the large pavilion tent that housed the brothers of the Order.

From behind him came the sudden sound of running footsteps. Before he could turn around, Oliver was struck by something heavy at the base of his neck, and he dropped senseless to the ground.

## Chapter Six
### RUADHAN

Ruadhan's thoughts, had he known it, were running along much the same lines as Oliver's. He, too, set aside the complicated questions about his feelings for the English knight and instead tried to focus on the issue of the murder of the Venetian silversmith.

Ruadhan sat bolt upright and said to himself, alarmed, "Peter Thistle!" Before he could do or say anything else, however, a series of shouts broke the camp's silence.

"What on Earth?" cried Hugh Thomas, just waking up, but Ruadhan was already sprinting towards the sounds of the disturbance. Several torches had been lit, and a great many people had gathered in one section of the camp. As Ruadhan ran, he heard snatches of people's talk - "The English knight! Sir Oliver has been slain!" – and felt his heart sink.

Ruadhan broke through a circle of people to see Oliver lying stretched out on the ground, and for a brief, heart-stopping moment, Ruadhan feared that the man was dead. Then, another figure forced his way through the crowd and knelt beside Oliver's head. It was Simon, Oliver's servant.

The servant looked closely at Oliver's face, touching a finger to his lips. He looked up at Ruadhan with an expression of relief and said, "He breathes, milord."

The Templar sent a silent prayer of thanks up to heaven and said, "God be praised. Lift him up and carry him to our tent."

Simon shook his head. "What if his neck is injured, milord? We may do him worse harm."

Hugh and the other Templars arrived. "What has happened here?" Hugh demanded.

"My master has been struck down, milord. He is unconscious, and we do not know what harm he has taken," said Simon.

"Who found him?" said Hugh.

"I did, Brothers," said a sturdily built pilgrim at the front of the crowd. "I heard a scuffle outside my tent and the sound of a blow. I grabbed my dagger and left my tent, ready to drive off any ruffians. Instead, I found this man lying in the dirt and no one else to be seen. He is the English knight, is he not?"

"He is," said Hugh. "What was he doing so far from his own tent in the middle of the night?"

"It is quite possible that he had the same thought that I did, Brother Hugh," said Ruadhan. "It had just occurred to me, not moments ago, that with the exception of one man, everyone who spoke with the Venetian silversmith has died. That man's life may be also in danger."

Hugh stared at him for a moment, then said, "Peter Thistle." Turning to the crowd, he called, "If anyone knows the whereabouts of Peter, sometimes known as Peter Thistle, let them come forward!"

"Why, his tent is next to mine, Brothers," said the sturdy

pilgrim who had discovered Oliver. He frowned. "I am amazed that he has not come out in response to all this commotion."

"Open the tent please, Brother Bernard," said Hugh quietly.

The Templar bent to his task, untying the fastenings and opening the front flap. He looked back at the others in astonishment. "He is gone, Brother. There is no trace of the man."

Eventually, the Templar sergeants moved Oliver's unconscious body off the ground, moving with great care under Simon's watchful eye. The servant would not be parted from his master, and when the sergeants placed Oliver on some blankets under the Templar's pavilion, Simon took up residence as if he belonged there.

"The waters of this affair become muddier with every passing moment," said Hugh. "I cannot make heads nor tails of tonight's events."

"Surely the case against Sir Oliver has become more serious?" pressed Gautier. "Last night the Englishman goes wandering at the same time a man is murdered. Tonight, he goes wandering, and at the same time, a man disappears."

"What are you suggesting, Brother Gautier?" asked Ruadhan angrily. "Oliver kidnapped a man who somehow managed to disappear and knock Oliver unconscious simultaneously?"

"His behaviour has been suspicious," insisted Gautier.

"No more than yours," Ruadhan shot back.

Gautier's eyes narrowed, but before anything further could be said, Hugh said firmly, "Hold, Brothers, enough! This is unseemly. Whatever our disagreements may be, outsiders must see us as one united body. Brother Gautier, the Englishman appears to be more the victim of a crime than a perpetrator.

Brother Ruadhan, the man owes us an answer as to why he has been wandering at night. Let us wait until morning. If Sir Oliver has not awoken before then, we must try to rouse him. In the meantime, let the sergeants search for this Peter Thistle."

---

Ruadhan sat on a stone and moodily watched the fire, trying to order his thoughts. The reason for Oliver's wandering seemed straightforward; like Ruadhan, the Englishman had realized that the cooper's life might be in danger. Therefore, Oliver had gone to find him. But who had struck Oliver down? And where was Peter bloody Thistle?

"I know why you defend him."

The hairs on the back of Ruadhan's neck went up as Gautier sat beside him.

Gautier smiled at him. "The Englishman is very fair, isn't he? That thatch of blond hair, those apple cheeks. A strong body. Powerful thighs, I would imagine."

Ruadhan sat absolutely stock still. Finally, he said, "What a vivid imagination you have, Brother Gautier."

"Oh, no imagination," replied Gautier easily. "I even stole a kiss from him at the Red Tower the other night. Wonderfully soft lips."

Ruadhan concentrated all his energies on keeping his face still. "Am I your confessor, Brother Gautier?"

"As if I would confess to *you*," sneered Gautier. "You hypocrite. All that I have done is all that you desperately wish to do and more. I've seen the way you look at the Englishman. We've all seen it. You think you're better than me? I just do the things that you are too frightened to do."

The French knight put his lips close to Ruadhan's ear and whispered, "You will never stop paying for refusing me. I will make you pay, and pay, and pay."

Then he was gone.

Ruadhan waited for the span of ten heartbeats, then slowly exhaled. He put his head in his hands.

"That man is not only a bully but a liar, milord," said Simon, stepping from the shadows into the firelight. "Those two traits often walk hand in hand. Unfortunately, he is neither a coward nor a fool, making him dangerous."

"Did you hear all that passed between us?" demanded Ruadhan.

"Everything except for whatever he whispered into your ear, milord," replied Simon. "You will forgive me, I hope. My master is in danger and has no one to look out for him, save me. I do my duty by keeping a weather eye on those who would seek to harm him, and by giving counsel to those who would help him, milord." Simon took a stick and rearranged the wood on the fire.

"So, you heard him talking about...kissing Sir Oliver," managed Ruadhan. He found it very hard to get the words out, and his stomach was knotted with tension.

Simon stopped rearranging logs on the fire and looked Ruadhan directly in the eyes. "My lord," he said clearly. "I have served Sir Oliver since he was very young. I know exactly who he is. I see how he looks at you and how you look at him. I am not blind. And I hope you are not such a fool as to imagine that Sir Oliver would ever kiss that snake of man. Milord." He turned back to the fire.

Ruadhan was pale with shock. Finally, he managed, "And knowing this about your master...it doesn't...I mean, you don't..."

"Do not judge, or you too will be judged. For in the same way you judge others, you will be judged, and with the measure you use, it will be measured to you," said Simon.

Ruadhan stared at the man, dumbstruck.

"The gospel according to Matthew, milord," said Simon.

There was a soft moan. Simon swiftly turned from the fire and peered into the darkness. "God be praised," he murmured. "My master wakes. Come with me, milord," he said to Ruadhan. "He will be glad to see you."

Ruadhan, still in a fog, followed the servant to where Oliver lay. The English knight was dreadfully pale, but Simon raised his head and gave him water.

"Simon," said Oliver in a dry and gravelly voice, "do me a favour, and get the name of the ship that docked on my head. Oh, hello, Ruadhan. I don't suppose you have any idea what happened to me?"

"I was about to ask you the same question," replied Ruadhan. The relief he felt at seeing Oliver awake made his heart light. "I don't suppose you saw who struck you?"

"I can only wish," said Oliver. "Remembering things feels like grabbing at mist." His eyes grew wide. "Peter Thistle!" he cried. "We have to find the man," he said, struggling to get up.

Ruadhan laid a hand on the knight's chest. "Gently, my friend, gently. You are not well, and Peter Thistle is nowhere to be found. You were discovered unconscious outside the man's tent, practically, but it was empty." Ruadhan gently increased his pressure on Oliver's chest, and slowly, the man laid back down.

"I was?" asked Oliver. "That's a laugh. I had no idea where the man was, and I was on my way to find you hoping you had some idea. That's like looking for a serpent and stepping into its nest."

The colour was slowly returning to Oliver's cheeks. Ruadhan leaned back as Simon gave his master some more water.

"Thank you, Simon. It feels like the same serpent whose nest I stepped in shat in my mouth. God, that's a tortured metaphor. I must have been hit harder than I thought."

"Milord," said Simon, "you would do well to ease your words and rest your mind."

"That's his way of telling me to shut up," said Oliver, smiling. "Very well. Ruadhan, would you mind telling me what I have missed?"

"There is not a great deal to say," answered Ruadhan. He had to restrain himself from the urge to stroke Oliver's fair hair. The Englishman looked very vulnerable, which made Ruadhan feel protective. "You were discovered after you had been knocked out. There was a great hue and cry. Brother Hugh demanded that Peter Thistle be brought to him, and his tent was discovered to be both close to you and quite empty." Ruadhan paused, then said, "Brother Gautier has implied that your behaviour is suspicious and that you were seen wandering in the camp both tonight and on the night that Arnaldo the silversmith was murdered."

"Hah! He should know. That slimy fellow was about some business of his own the night Arnaldo was murdered." Oliver eyed Ruadhan. "There is something you should know. Gautier found me that night by the well and had words for me. He tried to seduce me. Well, not exactly. He made it very clear that he wanted me to seduce him. He was not happy when I rejected him."

There was a brief silence then Ruadhan said, "He told me that you two had kissed."

Oliver swore. "Of course, he did. What a little weasel. No, Ruadhan. Nothing happened. It's important to me that you know that." He reached out and grasped the Templar's hand.

Ruadhan took Oliver's hand in his. It was a strong hand, sword-callused and firm, but Oliver's grip was gentle. Ruadhan looked into the Englishman's eyes and found only honesty and tenderness there.

There was a clatter from behind them, and both men jerked away in surprise.

"Forgive my clumsiness, milords," said Simon. "I must have dropped something. Ah, here come Brother Hugh and the other Templars."

"A pox on your clumsiness, Simon," said Oliver, but his tone belied his words. "Brother Templars," he said, straightening up. "Forgive me. I would greet you more properly, but my legs are shakier than a heretic on holy ground."

"A poor choice of words," said Gautier disapprovingly.

"If you will, but wait until my head is clear, Brother Gautier, you may find that I have some better words for you," replied Oliver.

"Enough," said Hugh impatiently. "I would ask that both of you mind your tongues."

"You may hold sway over your own man, Brother Hugh, but I do not recall having taken an oath of obedience myself," said Oliver, his tone low and dangerous. "I keep my own counsel where my honour is concerned, thank you."

"Then will you curb yourself for the sake of finding justice? Consider this a humble and courteous request," said Hugh.

"I will guard my tongue to the same degree that this fellow looks after his own," replied Oliver.

"Reasonable enough," said Hugh, with a warning glance at Gautier, who flushed. "Sir Oliver, we are glad to find you have recovered your wits. Can you identify the person who struck you?"

"Alas, I cannot, Brothers. I was struck from behind and did not see my attacker."

"May I ask how you came to be beside Peter Thistle's tent?" asked Hugh.

"Entirely by chance, Brother Hugh. I was travelling from my resting place to your pavilion, in the hopes of discovering where Peter Thistle made his bed. If you can picture the whole of the camp in your mind, you will see that I travelled in a straight line from my tent towards your own," replied Oliver.

Hugh looked at his fellow Templars. Bernard nodded. "It is true."

"So, you have no idea as to the current whereabouts of Peter Thistle?" pressed Hugh.

"Brothers, I am just as keen to find this man as you are," said Oliver. "It would seem to me that if anyone can give an account of the strange doings of the past two days, he is the man to do so."

"I am loath to commit any Brothers to the task of finding this man," said Hugh. "This caravan has already been attacked once already, and we may have sore need of men to protect them."

"Then I will go," said Oliver. "I am under no one's command and may go as I please. Keep your brothers here to guard the caravan."

"This is not your land, Sir Oliver," objected Hugh. "Would you even be able to find the caravan once you had left it?"

"Not to mention the fact that your own actions are under question," sneered Gautier.

Oliver said nothing, but simply looked at Hugh.

"Brother Gautier, you have already been asked once to curb your tongue," said Hugh, red-faced and looking irritable. "There will be consequences to my having to remind you of this. Sir Oliver is under no one's suspicion," Hugh continued with heavy emphasis. "Nevertheless, it seems wise that someone join him, if only to ensure that he does not lose his way. Brother Ruadhan, please join Sir Oliver in searching for Peter Thistle, and look to return to us with some answer to this strange set of affairs."

Ruadhan nodded. "Very well, Brother Hugh."

"You will need to leave your entourage of sergeants with us," the senior Templar continued, "we cannot afford to lose their numbers."

"My man Simon will join us," said Oliver. "He has the strength of ten because his heart is pure. Well, mostly pure."

"Brother Hugh, I must protest this decision!" cried Gautier.

"Brother Gautier, one more word from you, and you will be taken back to the Acre commandery in chains," said Hugh, stone-faced, "even though we can ill afford to lose the men. Do you truly want to be responsible for this?"

Gautier finally held his tongue.

"Draw an extra horse for each of you," Hugh went on as if nothing had happened. "Have your man take additional stores from our supplies, Sir Oliver, and plenty of water. Brother Ruadhan will carry the authority of the Order with him should any question you."

Hugh put his hand on Ruadhan's shoulder. "Brother, you know well that it is rare for a member of the Order to be sent on any mission without another Brother at his side. Be mindful that you carry the honour of the Poor Knights of Christ with you."

Ruadhan wondered why Hugh had felt it necessary to speak thusly in front of everyone but simply inclined his head and murmured, "Of course, Brother."

"Well then," said Hugh, looking around at the others, "it's unlikely that there will be any further sleep in this camp. We might as well regain some of the time we lost yesterday. Brother Ruadhan, is there aught else you need from us?"

Ruadhan thought quickly. "A bow, perhaps? We may need to hunt to supplement our stores."

"Three bows, all told," interjected Oliver. "Simon and I are English, after all, and no stranger to the bow."

"Very well," said Hugh, nodding. "Draw them when you draw supplies. And good hunting, gentleman. May we see you in Jerusalem before too long."

"Without doubt," replied Oliver. "Simon has never tried to murder me in my sleep, but if we miss seeing the Holy City, my nights will not be safe."

Hugh smiled uncertainly and left them to their preparations, taking the other Templars with him. Ruadhan did not miss the venomed look Gautier shot them.

"You know, I'm beginning to think that Brother Gautier is not as attracted to me as he said he was," pronounced Oliver.

Ruadhan quickly glanced around them. "Mind your tongue, for our Saviour's sake!" he muttered fiercely. "A camp is a terrible place for rumours."

"What is it with you Templars and telling me to be quiet?" demanded Oliver querulously. "I can tell you; it's starting to wear thin."

"You do not want to be the subject of camp gossip," said Ruadhan.

Oliver shook his head. "If I feared camp gossip, I would be a very different person to the one I am," he said.

"I can attest to that, milord," said Simon.

"Alright, you can definitely mind *your* tongue, Simon," said Oliver.

"Yes, milord."

---

Their preparations were complete before half of an hour had passed, and the three men were ready to go before the rest of the camp had finished all of their packing. Their speed was fortunate because they still needed to determine the direction Peter Thistle had taken away from camp, and they would have little hope of finding the man's tracks once the caravan was on the move.

"Here, milords." Simon, on foot and leading his horse, lowered his torch to show the knights a set of tracks.

"How can you be sure?" asked Ruadhan with a frown.

"The man was wearing leather boots with a thick sole, milord," replied Simon. "They match the prints you see here."

"You noticed that?" Ruadhan asked in surprise.

"I did indeed, milord," replied Simon. "I was a...forester before I was a servant to the Oakeshott family."

"Come along, Simon," said Oliver, "Ruadhan is a friend and may be trusted. Simon's first career was as a poacher, and he was the curse of three counties. When he was finally caught, it was my father who saved him from having his eyes put out."

"The Oakeshott family has been very kind to me, milords,"

acknowledged Simon, his blush clear in the torchlight. "If you look closely, milords, you will see that these tracks continue straight to the north. I do not know how far I will be able to follow them by torchlight, but we can certainly begin."

"Once the sun rises, will you be able to follow the tracks while on horseback?" asked Oliver.

"I cannot promise, but I think so, milord," replied Simon.

"Then we stand a decent chance of catching him before a second nightfall," said Oliver with satisfaction.

"God willing," said Ruadhan.

## Chapter Seven
### OLIVER

Their pace was sedate through the predawn hours. Simon was confident but cautious, not wanting to lead them astray. As he had warned, he could only follow the tracks on foot. Ruadhan had competently arranged their spare horses in a train, with the lead horse's reins tied to the horn of his saddle.

"Not the first time you've done that," observed Oliver as the Templar tied the last loop.

Ruadhan nodded. "The Ui Neills are well known for their horses," he said. "In my family, you were among them as soon as you had the wit not to walk beneath their hooves."

"Some learn faster than others, I would imagine," said Oliver.

Ruadhan nodded. "So they do. At least they did in my day. And in fairness, my cousin Ruraidh wasn't that bright even before a horse stepped on his head."

They both laughed.

"You know, I think this is the first time I've seen you talk of your home with a smile on your face," said Oliver. "Do you miss it? Or do you have memories that leave a sour taste?"

"Large questions before the sun has even risen in the sky," observed Ruadhan after a pause.

"Let the darkness swallow my questions if I ask too much, and that will be an end to them," replied Oliver.

"Rather poetic, aren't you?" asked Ruadhan, bemused.

"It's the predawn air," said Oliver, "it makes everything sound more eloquent."

Ruadhan let out a sigh of exasperation. "Bless me, Oliver, I don't know why it's so difficult for me to get the words out. It's not really all that complicated."

"You don't need to say anything."

"I know," said Ruadhan, "but I'd like to try. I've just never spoken it aloud before, that's all."

They rode in silence for a while, the bent figure of Simon some ten yards or so ahead of them.

Finally, Ruadhan said, "I don't know about your Oakeshotts, Oliver, but the Ui Neills are a tight-knit bunch. Cousins upon cousins spread over the countryside, squabbles all over the place of course, but everybody pretty familiar with everybody else's business and always, always having an opinion on the comings and goings and doings of members of the family. No one shy about giving their opinion, either!"

Oliver laughed. "We're very different among the Oakeshotts. We're rather dour. At least, everyone who lives under my father's roof tends to watch their words. William Oakeshott casts a long shadow over the rest of the family. But that's neither here nor there; do go on."

"Well," Ruadhan continued, "as you can imagine, in a family

where everyone has an opinion on everything, there is much speculation on the status and futures of the unmarried Ui Neills, especially when – like me – they have reached a prime marrying age. The more time passes, the more questions are raised."

"Ah," said Oliver knowingly. "And questions were being raised about you."

"They were indeed. Various and sundry plans had been made about my match since I was born, and the general consensus was fixed upon one Rosamund O'Fearghal, a decent enough woman whom I had known for more than half of my life. Of course, I had no interest in Rosamund, not that way."

Oliver nodded. This was unspoken territory between them, and he was trying to navigate it carefully. Neither of them had been overt, but the connection between them was obvious. That being said, Oliver had been in situations where such feelings had disappeared like morning mist if the wrong thing was said, or even the right thing too soon.

"So there I was, Oliver," Ruadhan continued. "There had always been rumors about me; little enough because I was discreet. But I knew that as I grew older, more tongues would wag. One friend in the know suggested that I marry Rosamund anyway and just live the life I wanted within the safety of a marriage. Goodness knows it's been done many times before. But I liked Rosamund and saw no reason why she should suffer for a lack that was no fault of her own."

"Not an easy situation," agreed Oliver.

"No. I had a choice to make. Did I join the clergy? Again, it's been done many times before, of course, and it is not a bad life to be found in the cloister if you are wealthy enough. But life in a monastery would mean I would never pick up shield and lance again, and that thought was unbearable."

"I understand," said Oliver. "I would sooner give up breathing than put down my sword."

"I know," said Ruadhan. "I saw that when I saw you fight; you feel it, too. 'Battle-joy,' my ancestors called it. That fierce passion that runs through you when the rest of the world disappears, and all that matters is the next heartbeat, the next swing, and then the one after that." The Irishman's face was flushed, and he stared off into the distance. "It's when I feel most alive," he admitted.

Oliver's heart swelled. It was as if his heart's desire was being breathed out through another man's mouth. Ruadhan had captured exactly the feelings that suffused Oliver's body when he was in the heat of battle and the clarity he found there.

"Please believe me," said Oliver, his voice thick, "when I tell you that I share everything that you have just said."

Ruadhan's gaze turned from the horizon, his rainwater-blue eyes piercing Oliver's heart. He smiled. "I know you do," the Templar said, "I know."

They looked deeply into each other's eyes, and then the moment passed like a wave retreating from its high-water mark.

"So that is why you chose the Templars," Oliver said. "A vow of celibacy, removing any question of marriage, but a life of battle."

Ruadhan nodded. "Exactly that. I joined the local commandery and saw my way East to Outremer as soon as was possible. I was fortunate. I could have been assigned to a post in the middle of nowhere, garrisoning a castle in the northern Principality of Antioch or some such. Instead, I was sent to the Kingdom of Jerusalem and for the past year, have been quartered in Acre, escorting pilgrims to and from the Holy City."

"How has it been?" asked Oliver. "Joining the Order, I mean."

"A good life, take it for all in all," said Ruadhan, considering the question. "The fighting is as disciplined as anything I've ever seen. That's what comes when you have a group of knights under a vow of obedience. I live as well as I used to back in Ireland, and I never have to worry about where my next meal is coming from. You don't get to choose those that you live with, but then again, I never had that choice with my family either. Rivalries and jealousies crop up, as does a certain amount of bullying, but aside from that snake Gautier de Mesnil it's never been a problem for me."

"Ah, Gautier," said Oliver, "truly a piece of weasel shit. What is that bastard's problem?"

Ruadhan gave Oliver a sideways glance. "Surely you have met his type before."

"Possibly. What type is that?" returned the English knight.

Ruadhan hesitated. "Predatory," he said finally. "A man whose taste is not only for other men but also cannot understand why he should ever be refused."

"I see," replied Oliver. "Yes, I certainly got a taste of that from him." He paused. "I take it that you have as well."

"When I first came to Outremer," said Ruadhan, sighing. "I don't know if Gautier is uncommonly skilled at sniffing out men who are like you and me, or if he just doesn't care. At any rate, he was after me from very early on. Got me alone, propositioned me. I refused him, and he has cursed my steps ever since."

"I do know the type," admitted Oliver. "A fellow like that was part of the reason I had to leave England."

"A Templar?" asked Ruadhan.

"A bishop," chuckled Oliver.

"No!"

"In truth, the uproar with that old pervert was the proverbial last straw," said Oliver. "I was never indiscreet, but I was never exactly shy, either. I've always had the tendency to talk my way into trouble and fight my way out of it. The results turned out to be a little hotter than polite society in England could bear."

"I can only imagine," said Ruadhan with a laugh. "The way you talk about the Holy Land and the faith, I'm amazed it hasn't put you in front of a religious examination before now."

"Does it bother you?" asked Oliver. "I've given offense to you before, I know."

"That you're less religious than me? It surprised me at first, I think; put me off balance. I'm a member of a religious order; when I'm not out on patrol, I'm at prayer three times a day or more. Every day, I'm surrounded with at least the outward show of a constant devotion to God."

"What about you, Ruadhan?" Oliver pressed. "Are you very religious?"

"Yes, as it happens," replied Ruadhan. "Does that surprise you?"

"Somewhat," admitted Oliver.

"Why?"

"I have not found strong religious faith to be common among men like us," said Oliver. "Having to hide part of who you are, it tends to make men use religion as a kind of protective camouflage. People can be very good at the outward show of devotion because they have to be, but there has been very little sincere belief behind it. Just a lot of hypocrisy, like my bishop, who warned his flock against the dangers of lust and tried to have it off with me in the cathedral sacristy."

"Point taken," said Ruadhan. "I've seen my share of hypocrisy as well; I'll not deny it. But I do not put my faith in men. I put my faith in God. God is love, Oliver, and if I have love in my heart, it comes straight from the Most High."

Oliver shook his head.

"What?" demanded Ruadhan.

Oliver lifted his hand and counted on his fingers. "One, that's a beautiful thing to believe. Two, I think that I want to believe that myself. Three, if anyone here would be found guilty of heresy, it's not me, Master Irishman."

Ruadhan laughed. "You spoke earlier of protective camouflage. What I have shared with you is the belief of my heart. My outward show is the same as my brother Templars."

"So, what you have told me could get you into a lot of trouble," teased Oliver lightly.

"Who would believe the godless Englishman?" Ruadhan threw back at him.

---

The morning sky was beginning to lighten, and Simon continued to follow the tracks of the elusive Peter Thistle diligently. In the pre-dawn, they stopped to have a drink of water and to allow Simon a break from his difficult task.

"It seems to me that this fellow has been pretty consistent in travelling due North," said Oliver reflectively. "Is that fair to say, Simon?"

"Yes, milord." Simon took a deep drink from his canteen and returned it to his saddle bag.

"Have we gained on him at all?" asked Ruadhan.

"Difficult to say, milord. Once the sun is up, I may have a clearer answer," replied the servant.

"If we're still on the trail by noon, we'll want to leave it long enough to get water." Ruadhan pointed to a set of hills in the distance, silhouetted against the lightening sky. "There's a spring at the base of those hills. Next water to the north is a day's ride or more."

"Your knowledge of the lay of the land is impressive," said Oliver as he put his own canteen away.

"The first survival skill you learn here," replied Ruadhan. "If you don't learn it, you won't have the chance to learn anything else."

They rode through the breaking dawn, and the heat of the day began to slowly build. Their pace was faster once Simon was able to read Peter's tracks from horseback, and the three of them made steady time through the first hour of daylight. Suddenly, Simon threw up a hand for them to stop, cursing under his breath.

"What is it, Simon?" asked Oliver, tugging on his horse's reins.

"I would ask you to stop and not dismount, lords," answered Simon. "Keep your horses clear, if you please." Oliver's servant slipped from his horse and walked carefully around in a widening circle, stopping to double back twice. Then he jogged forward some thirty yards before returning to the waiting knights.

"Peter Thistle is no longer on foot, lords," announced Simon. "He was met here by three riders, who brought an extra horse with them. All four horses rode away together, heading back toward the coast."

"Back to Acre?" asked Ruadhan with a frown.

"I believe further north, milord. Towards Tyre, if they do not change their course," replied Simon.

"Blast," murmured Oliver. "So much for a quick chase."

"I do not like what this implies," said Ruadhan, still frowning.

"Go on," prompted Oliver.

"Look at this place. We're in the middle of nowhere, far from the road and perhaps half a day from water. No one meets here by chance."

"True enough," Oliver agreed. "This meeting must have been pre-arranged."

"Which suggests that everything that has happened so far has gone according to someone's schedule," said Ruadhan. "Arnaldo's murder, at least. Possibly the deaths of the boy and his mother?"

"Hold on," replied Oliver doubtfully. "You're running ahead of things, I think. We can't know that for certain, and assuming things can take us down the wrong path. All we know for sure is that Peter Thistle left the camp last night and met three people who were waiting here, possibly for him."

Ruadhan nodded. "That's fair. I keep wanting to see a pattern here, so much so that I'm trying to will one into existence. I don't like puzzles that remain out of my grasp."

"Subtle plans are certainly not my strong suit," said Oliver with a grin. "Simon, will you be able to follow the trail of these riders?"

"I should, milord. They are not trying to conceal themselves."

"Then let us carry on. At noon, if we have nothing else new to go on, we can break from the trail long enough to refresh our water."

The three men continued at a steady pace as the countryside shifted from scrub brush and dusty waste towards more arable land, even passing an orchard. It was still spring, long before harvest time, but the trees were beginning to sprout green buds and leaves.

"What kind of trees are these?" asked Oliver.

"Orange trees," replied Ruadhan absently, scanning the rows.

"What are you looking for?"

"A farmer who might have seen four riders," said Ruadhan. "Ah. Hang on. Let's try not to scare the fellow." The Templar called out to a man some distance away, in a language Oliver did not understand. Oliver kept his distance while the two conversed. Finally, Ruadhan waved to the farmer and rejoined Oliver and Simon.

"What did you discover?" asked Oliver.

"Little enough," answered Ruadhan. "Yes, he saw four riders, and yes, we are heading in the right direction if we wish to follow them. No, he was not close enough to see what they looked like, and no, he doesn't know if they were Christian, Saracen, or Jew."

"Cautious fellow," chuckled Oliver.

"Scared, I think," said Ruadhan reflectively, "and not of us."

"My lords?" interjected Simon.

"Yes, esteemed servant?" replied Oliver.

"If there is an orchard here, lords, there must be a supply of water. We could fill our canteens and refresh the horses without a long detour."

"Bless my soul, Simon, you're absolutely right," said Ruadhan. "Hold on, I'll talk to this fellow again and find out what's what." The Templar trotted through the orchard to find the farmer.

When he returned, Oliver asked him, "What language were you speaking to that man, anyhow?"

"Arabic," replied Ruadhan. "There's an irrigation canal at the far end of the orchard and a well next to it with clean water. We can let the horses drink and refill our canteens."

"You speak Arabic?" said Oliver, astonished.

"Stay here long enough. You'll pick up some as well," said Ruadhan.

"So that farmer was a Saracen?"

Ruadhan shrugged. "There's not enough Christians in the kingdom to work the land. They farm in peace as long as they pay their taxes and don't cause trouble. Well, that fellow does anyway." They approached the irrigation canal and dismounted, leading their horses to drink. Simon gathered their canteens and carried them to the well.

"So, there are Saracens living within the kingdom," said Oliver, shaking his head. "I saw none in Acre."

Ruadhan laughed. "How would you be able to tell? If there's a secret to telling the difference between a Shi'ite or a Sunni or a Maronite or a Jacobite, nobody's ever told me."

"You're making those words up," accused Oliver.

Ruadhan laughed harder. "I swear I'm not. Let's just say that there is nothing simple in Outremer. I have seen the Arabs of Damascus make common cause with Christian princes to fight against the Seljuks of Baghdad, or the Rum up in the north. I have heard old men say that the Christians would never have captured the great city of Antioch if the local Saracen lords had not been fighting amongst themselves. Outremer is a strange place."

"I would have never guessed that from Acre," Oliver admitted. "It seemed little different from a half dozen other cities on the shores of the Mediterranean."

"That's because Acre is thick with Christians from the west," said Ruadhan. "The Venetians have a quarter. So do the Pisans and the Genoese. Then there is the Templar district and the Hospitaller district. The Saracens were squeezed out of Acre ten years ago or more."

"What about Jerusalem?" asked Oliver.

"Much the same. There was a massive slaughter when Jerusalem was taken, and the city has been slow to fill ever since. No Saracens or Jews are allowed within the city walls, and the Eastern Christians have been slow to return. The conquerors of Jerusalem did not scruple to ask the city's inhabitants about their faith when they broke the walls."

"Sounds like a boring place," observed Oliver.

"The centre of a kingdom's power will never be boring," responded Ruadhan. "Plus, the volume of pilgrim traffic is enormous. And, of course, for the religiously minded, the sites of Our Lord's miracles are something wondrous all by themselves," he added drily.

"Right. Forgot about that," said Oliver sheepishly. "Have you seen them, then?"

"I have. Seeing the lamps in the Holy Sepulchre lit on Easter morning is a sight to remember," said Ruadhan. "Among many other things. Sometimes, you suddenly realize that you are treading the very ground that Jesus and His apostles walked over a thousand years ago. It can be deeply moving."

"I'm sure," said Oliver, nodding.

"Get away with you," laughed Ruadhan. "I'd be more likely to find you wandering the Street of Bad Cookery."

"That's a real street?" asked Oliver, incredulous.

"The name is ironic. You will find some of the best food in Outremer on the Street of Bad Cookery."

Oliver shook his head. "I don't understand this place at all."

"Milords, I think the horses are as full as they can safely be," said Simon, "and our canteens are replenished once more."

---

The three men rode through the rising heat of the day, with Simon leading the way. A few times, they hit particularly rocky terrain, and Oliver's servant had to cast about to rediscover the trail, but the tracks did not deviate from a straight line to the city of Tyre.

As the sun was at its highest point, Ruadhan found them shelter in a small ring of trees and ordered a rest for the sake of the horses. Their mounts and spares were given water and the chance to crop at the vegetation that grew among the trees.

"There must be a source of water," said the Templar, peering around, "but it may well be underground and out of reach."

"You see, this is why I never left Acre," said Oliver, wiping the sweat from his eyes. "I've never seen such a parched land."

"It changes as you move further north," replied Ruadhan. "But yes, this is a dry and dusty place. The lands around the river Jordan are beautiful, as are the lands on the coast, but the space between the river and sea can be very dangerous for travellers, and pilgrims especially."

They remounted and resumed their journey.

"Simon, do you have any idea how far ahead they might be?" called Oliver.

"Difficult to say, milord. Horse droppings suggest a few hours at most."

"Should we spur the horses?" Oliver asked Ruadhan, but the Templar shook his head.

"A dangerous and uncertain business. I'd hate to lose a horse, and it may accomplish nothing. We know where they're going if their course holds true to Tyre. If they change their direction, then we have this conversation again."

Oliver was unused to taking the commands of others, but Outremer was truly a foreign land, and Ruadhan assumed leadership with an easy and confident air. He quietly regarded the Irish Templar as they rode. The man had a good seat in the saddle and rode upright without seeming stiff-backed. He had broad shoulders, too, and carried a seemingly unconscious air of nobility, like he came from some long-forgotten line of Irish royalty.

There was much to admire about Ruadhan Ui Neill. He fought like a lion, was not easily cowed by enemy or bully, and if Oliver found Ruadhan's views on religion somewhat naïve, he still respected the man's sincerity and depth of faith. His face was like some stern angel out of the Old Testament, and his blue eyes would sometimes flash with the man's amusement or disapproval. Either way, they cut Oliver to the core.

*Is there a chance of something here?* Oliver asked himself, and he was met with his own mixture of hope and doubt. He was drawn to the man, finding him compelling and physically beautiful. Coupled with that, Oliver knew that Ruadhan was looking at him in much the same manner. Desire was mingled with fear, however; beginnings so delicate that Oliver did not wish to jeopardize the connection they shared by being too hasty or forward.

When Ruadhan had been standing among the trees, rubbing down his horse, Oliver had wanted nothing more than to stride forward, take the Irishman's head in his hands, and bring it down to discover if the man's lips tasted as beautiful as they looked. The close presence of Simon had been a deterrent, but even more than that was the fear that Ruadhan would look at him in that moment and Oliver would see remorse. Or regret. Or anything that might constitute a rejection.

If that happened, it was hard for Oliver to imagine how they could continue to journey together. And more than anything else, Oliver wanted, terribly wanted, to remain in the Templar's company. He wanted to hear Ruadhan laugh again, see how it brought out the lines in the Irishman's face that broke his stern countenance so that you could see a childish joy. He wanted to be the one that made Ruadhan laugh.

Above all, Oliver wanted to see the man fight again. The Englishman loved combat more than anything else in the world; utterly lost himself in it, was obsessed by it, and had never found an equal. He genuinely did not know if he could defeat Ruadhan. Part of him wanted to find out. Another part of him wanted to fight alongside the man against all comers.

"Lords? We have a problem," called Simon. Oliver and Ruadhan caught up to him, and the problem was plain to see. Two sets of hoofprints continued northwest towards Tyre, and two sets split off and turned to the northeast.

"I don't suppose there's any way to tell which horse Peter is riding?" Oliver asked hopefully.

Simon shook his head. "No way at all, milord."

"Damn," said Ruadhan softly, "damn and blast. Either we split up, which has its own problems, or we must choose." He straightened. "Thoughts?"

Oliver considered. "Simon is the best tracker by a mile, and you're the one who knows where the water is. Any way we split it, we lose someone that both groups would need. I say we have to choose a path and stick to it. Simon?"

"I agree, milord."

Ruadhan nodded. "Can't argue with that logic. So which path do we choose?"

"I've always wanted to see Tyre," offered Oliver.

Ruadhan smiled. "Liar. You never wanted to leave Acre."

"I've always wanted to see Tyre since we talked about it today," said Oliver.

The Irish knight laughed. "Fair enough. I couldn't tell you why, but my instinct says Tyre as well. Simon?"

"I agree, lords."

"Stop being so contrary, Simon," demanded Oliver. "Your disagreeable nature is tearing this group apart."

"Yes, milord."

"Tyre it is, then," said Oliver.

# Chapter Eight
## RUADHAN

Their pursuit continued over the next two days without incident. They lost the trail when it joined the main road going west to the coastal city, but by that point, they were less than half a day's travel away from Tyre itself. Simon kept an eye on tracks leading away from the road, just in case their quarry had tried to use the road to conceal another destination, but could find nothing.

As Oliver had put it, sometimes you just needed to grab your balls and go.

Now they had reached the shacks and tents of the Foregate, the area in front of the city walls where those who could not live within the city would gather. The dwellings reached all the way to the sea, but the massive causeway that connected the mainland to the city on the water was kept clear.

"Impressive," said Oliver as they cleared the community of the Foregate and surveyed the causeway. "Be a bastard of a city to take. One way in and one way out, and no way to lay siege unless you controlled the waters as well."

"Apparently it used to be even tougher," said Ruadhan.

"According to history, Tyre used to be a separate island just off the coast. Alexander the Great built this causeway to connect the city to the mainland so that he could attack it."

"What couldn't that man do," said Oliver appreciatively. "So how the devil did we pry it out of the hands of the Saracens?"

"Same answer as the rest of the coastal cities," replied Ruadhan. "Did a deal with the Venetians for their support from the sea. And the Pisans, and the Genoese as well."

"Does that mean they all have quarters in this city as well?" asked Oliver in astonishment. "How does the kingdom make any money with those greedy bastards plucking every penny they can get their hands on?"

"Fortunately, there are many pennies to be plucked," said Ruadhan dryly. He eyed his companion. "Am I going to have any trouble with you getting into fights with Venetian dice-throwers?"

Oliver held up a hand and did his best to put on a devout face. "Not a bit of it. I'm on a sacred mission in the company of a man sworn to God's service."

Ruadhan rolled his eyes. "Heaven help us all. Simon, watch your master like a hawk, will you?"

"I'll try, milord."

---

Entry to the city was easy enough, especially since Ruadhan wore the surcoat of the Poor Knights of Christ. The city guards wore the livery of the Queen of Jerusalem, the Lady Melisende.

"Is it just me, or does the monarchy hold all of the finest

cities in the kingdom?" asked Oliver as they rode through the massive gate. "Does this kingdom not have any high lords?"

Ruadhan chuckled. "Did you really just spend your time in Acre drinking and dicing?"

"Do you really need an answer to that?"

"Your lesson in politics will have to wait, I'm afraid. The Templar commandery is just inside the city walls, and we are here," said Ruadhan.

The sturdy Templar quarters were well within bowshot of the city gate itself, and the building dominated a space equivalent to a city block. The black and white standard of the Order flew at the top of one squat tower, whilst the familiar red cross on a white background flew at the top of another.

The trio dismounted and led their horses through the entrance of the commandery and into the forecourt. A stablemaster came forward and ordered his grooms to see to the horses.

"With your permission, lord," said Simon, and at Oliver's nod, he followed the grooms to ensure the horses were treated properly.

"Brother Ruadhan!" called a stocky knight in the surcoat of the Order, striding across the forecourt. "Well met. Your presence is a surprise; I thought you still patrolled the pilgrim road from Acre!" The knight enveloped Ruadhan in a powerful embrace.

"Well met, Brother Fabien," smiled Ruadhan after the man stepped back. "I am happy to see the Lord treating you well. I will tell you the reason for my arrival once we have the chance to sit down privately. But first, let me introduce you to Sir Oliver Oakeshott, a knight from England and my companion on this journey."

Fabien smiled at Oliver and clasped his arm firmly. "Well met, Sir Oliver. Any friend of Brother Ruadhan's is a friend of mine."

"You are very kind," replied Oliver, "and thank you for the hospitality. It's been a dusty few days."

"I can only imagine!" said Fabien. "I am sure you will both be refreshed by a nice cool bath. Why don't you do that, and then you can join me in my chambers."

"Baths!" exclaimed Oliver happily. "Before I came east of Constantinople, I might as well have never heard of them. Now, I would scandalize half of England with my bathing."

"If you didn't scandalize them over something else first," laughed Ruadhan. "Follow me! The Tyre commandery boasts the finest baths you will find in the kingdom."

The two men left the forecourt and soon travelled down a finely cut stone stairwell. "Mind your footing," warned Ruadhan as they rounded a corner. "The steam can make the floor slippery.

"Is it a hot spring?" asked Oliver as they reached an empty room, save for wooden benches and clothes pegs.

"No, they use water and heated stones," replied Ruadhan as he began to remove his clothing. "The real treat is the cold-water bath afterwards, the frigidarium. Fed straight from the sea. Jumping in after the steam bath, you will never feel more alive."

"Sounds like heaven to me!" laughed Oliver as he quickly stripped down. The Englishman was powerfully built, with remarkable definition in the muscles of his calves and thighs. His chest was broad and bore a collection of scars that was unusual for one so young.

Ruadhan swallowed. With the exception of the scars, Oliver's body was sweet and fresh, compact and powerful. He felt his arousal grow at the sight of it and quickly turned to go into the steam room so that Oliver would not notice.

He was not quick enough to avoid Oliver's hand firmly smacking Ruadhan's ass.

"Don't think I didn't catch you looking," laughed Oliver. Ruadhan made a strangled noise, then decided to say nothing at all.

The steam room featured benches against three walls, and in the middle of the room, a brazier full of stones over a hot fire, with a bucket of water and a ladle next to the brazier. Ruadhan filled the ladle with water and slowly poured it over the stones, producing a gratifying amount of steam.

"That's as good as medicine," sighed Oliver, leaning back on a bench. "More, Ruadhan, please."

Ruadhan was not sure if Oliver was deliberately teasing him, but he was having a difficult time not responding to the Englishman's sensuality, coupled with his nudity. Oliver seemed completely comfortable in his nakedness, and why not? The warrior had a splendid body and, if Ruadhan was not mistaken, was being openly tempting.

Ruadhan ladled more water onto the stones, raising more steam.

"Like heaven," moaned Oliver, lying on his back on his bench, his hands behind his head. To Ruadhan, he looked nothing short of magnificent.

The Irishman closed his eyes. To act on his feelings was unthinkable.

*Here, in a Templar commandery?*

If another brother walked through that door and caught them, his life would be over. Both of their lives.

Ruadhan wiped the sweat from his forehead and straightened. "And now, the cold water," he said. "Come on, you sluggard." He walked back into the changing room and took the other entrance. The condensation from the steam meeting the cold air of the frigidarium made the stones very slippery. "Mind yourself," he warned. There were steps leading into the cold-water pool, but Ruadhan ignored them and went to the side. Taking a deep breath, he jumped in.

The shock to his body was at first physically painful, then glorious. He gasped as he surfaced, the cold water forcing air from his lungs. Every part of his skin felt incredibly alive.

Ruadhan put a hand up to protect himself from the splash as Oliver jumped in after him. He laughed at the sight of Oliver's shocked face as the warrior surfaced, gasping. "God's wounds!" he cried, his chest working as he struggled to take in air. "That's like – that's like – I don't even know what that's like!"

"A rare pleasure," said Ruadhan, smiling.

An odd look came over Oliver's face, and he stared at the Irishman. "Yes," he said, finally, in a strangely vulnerable way.

In that moment, there was nothing more that Ruadhan wanted in the entire world than to kiss Oliver. Their eyes locked, and he knew that Oliver felt it, too. They moved slowly towards each other.

"There are towels for you, lords, in the changing room," said Simon, clearing his throat. "Brother Fabien is expecting you shortly."

Oliver gave a cough. "Thank you, Simon," he said. "We're just coming out. "Can you bring us a change of clothes, please?"

"Already done, milord. They are folded and waiting for you in the changing room."

"As prepared as ever, Simon."

"Yes, milord."

For a long moment, silence hung between Ruadhan and Oliver before the Englishman finally shook his head and swam towards the steps leading out of the cold-water pool. "Did you know that in the courts in Acre, the judge originally sentenced Simon to a whipping?" he asked, emerging naked from the water and walking into the changing room.

Ruadhan followed him, grabbing a towel from a peg and starting to dry off. "I'd heard that," he replied.

"At the time, allowing that to happen was unthinkable," said Oliver, towelling himself off. "An hour from now, I am sure it will be unthinkable again. But here and now," he growled, "well." He began to pull on the white cotton shift that had been left for him. "Well. That's all that I will say."

"Indeed," managed Ruadhan, pulling on his own shift. Then, his own impish spirit rose up in him, and he said, "We didn't even get the chance to rub each other down with sponges. Never mind the oil."

Oliver's jaw dropped, and Ruadhan deftly reached around to give the Englishman a firm smack on his ass before leaving the changing room.

---

A few minutes later saw them more fully clothed and seated in the Knight Commander's chambers, high up in the commandery building. Fabien poured them some ale and offered them a plate of grapes.

"Our vineyards are finally bearing fruit, I'm happy to say," said Fabien as he passed the plate around. "A few years, and we should be producing our vintages."

Ruadhan sipped at his ale. "I look forward to trying them, Brother Fabien," he said politely.

"We'll sell more than we keep, of course, but it's my hope that we'll make the local grapes famous," continued Fabien. "Brother Etienne comes from a wine-making family in Bourdeaux. He's been working wonders." The Templar commander sat down, leaving the plate of grapes on the table between Ruadhan and Oliver. "But you didn't come here to discuss the future of the *duri* grape," he said. "How can I assist you?"

Ruadhan leaned forward and gave Fabien a rough outline of the events that had brought them to Tyre. When he had finished, the commander frowned.

"There are a few threads in your tale that are worth picking up," he said. "Let me see if I can order them in my mind." Fabien absently popped a grape into his mouth. "First, we have certainly noticed more bandit activity in the countryside, no more than a day's ride from the city. It sounds as if you may be experiencing the start of this around Acre as well. Second, I've never heard of this Peter Thistle fellow, but we can ask around the city to see if anyone's heard of such a man who recently arrived in the city. How would you describe him?"

"Average height, slender build but very strong forearms, short black hair and a closely trimmed black beard, dark eyes," answered Ruadhan. "And he would have arrived on horseback with a companion."

"Not a man to stand out in a crowd," said Fabien dubiously. "How did you notice his forearms?"

"They were exceedingly muscled," said Ruadhan. "He said that he was a cooper, so I thought little of it."

"Hmm," murmured Fabien, reaching for another grape. "The third thing is this necklace he mentioned. The apple pendant made by Arnaldo, the murdered man? An unusual decoration."

"I thought so at the time," admitted Ruadhan.

"It stirs a memory in me," said Fabien, "but it's like a ticklish trout, just toying with the line. There's something there, but it will not let me bring it to the surface just yet. Let's hope that it will come in its own time." The commander rose to his feet. "We can host you in the barracks, of course, Brother Ruadhan, and I'm sure that we can find somewhere comfortable to accommodate you, Sir Oliver. We have a number of guests staying with us at the moment, so you may dine and pray with them."

"Our thanks, Brother Fabien," said Ruadhan as he and Oliver also rose. "I'm not sure how long we will be staying; Brother Hugh Thomas has placed me under the obligation to find Peter Thistle and fetch him back for questioning. If we cannot find him here, we will need to move on."

"Of course. We will pray for your success," said Fabien, escorting them out of his chambers.

Ruadhan wondered how long Oliver would manage to keep his silence. He lasted to the stairs back down to the forecourt.

"If I needed advice on vine clippings and soil cycles, I think I've found our man," said Oliver. "Or apples and their suitability as pendants. For a manhunt, however, I am less certain."

Ruadhan chuckled. "Don't sell Brother Fabien short," he said. "He may not give the impression of urgency, I must admit, but he is no man's fool."

"I'd feel better if we were looking for a rogue grape," grumbled Oliver. "I can't sit on my hands, Ruadhan. I'm going to walk about the city and have a nose about. Either Peter is here, or he chose the other path and makes distance on us with every hour."

"Don't go alone," said Ruadhan.

"My humble servant Simon shall join me," said Oliver, grinning. "With my soul in his care, how can I go astray?"

He clapped Ruadhan on the shoulder and strode off, shouting for Simon.

---

When the bell tolled for noontime prayers, Ruadhan joined his brother Templars in the commandery's chapel. The chapel was a simple affair, lit by windows set high in the stone walls. There was little enough stained glasswork in the churches of Outremer, but the chapel had a beautiful series behind the altar that portrayed the martyrdom of St. Sebastian. Ruadhan took his place in the pews and knelt, contemplating the courage that it must have taken for St. Sebastian to face the arrows of his oppressors and still sing the praises of God. Any time Ruadhan had been shot, he was armored and shielded. To be bound naked to a tree, waiting for the arrow's bite? Ruadhan wondered if he would have the bravery to sing his faith to the Lord under such circumstances.

*"Non nobis domine, non nobis, sed nomine tua da gloriam."*

Thus, the Templars began their prayer.

*"Not to us, Lord, not to us but to your name be the glory, because of your love and faithfulness. Why do the nations say, "Where is their God?" Our God is in heaven; he does whatever pleases him. But their idols are silver and gold, made by human hands."*

As his brothers continued to recite the 115th psalm, Ruadhan's mind broke from the track of the prayer, caught by the words.

*But their idols are silver and gold, made by human hands.*

Arnaldo the silversmith had not made a gift for the Canons of the Holy Sepulchre; Ruadhan was certain. He had made an idol of silver. But for what purpose?

It was at that point that the doors of the chapel slammed open, and the shouting began.

## Chapter Nine
### OLIVER

Oliver strode out of the Templar commandery, fiddling with his sword belt. "Damnation, this thing won't hang properly."

"Allow me, milord," said Simon, rearranging the hang of Oliver's surcoat. "That should be better."

"Thank you," said Oliver absently. His thoughts were entirely on Ruadhan and the moment they had shared – well, almost shared. He was certain that they had been within moments of sharing a kiss, and then, who knows? What would have happened if Simon had not arrived?

"Your timing," said Oliver, "Can leave something to be desired."

"Yes, milord. It was either going to be me or a Templar servant."

"Ah." Oliver nodded. "In that case, well done." Circumstances, always circumstances. He and Ruadhan had travelled in the countryside for days, but the first real moment between them had occurred in a place filled with potential interruptions. Was that accidental or intentional on Ruadhan's part? It hadn't felt that way, but the way the encounter had ended left Oliver filled with doubt.

"Where do you wish to go, milord?"

"Sorry," said Oliver, "woolgathering." He fussed with his sword belt once more, making sure it hung properly from his hips. "Well," he said, "I don't even know who I would ask about new arrivals to the city. Best leave that to the Templars. Arnaldo was a Venetian silversmith, was he not? It's not much of a thread, but at least it's something I can tug on. Let's find the Venetian quarter."

"The last time we spent time among the Venetians, it did not end well, milord," said Simon dubiously.

"Nonsense! We just won't throw dice with them, that's all."

---

It did not take long for the pair to find the Venetian quarter in the city of Tyre. As was customary, the Venetians had taken an area by the port, where they could ensure the smooth flow of trade goods to and from the city. They had their own customs house right on the docks and a market square not far away.

"How on earth does the kingdom make any money from trade if Venice pays no customs duty?" Oliver wondered.

"Nor does Genoa, or Pisa, or the other great trading cities, milord."

"Madness!" exclaimed Oliver. "Why would the kingdom allow it?"

"I do not know, milord."

"Well, thank the heavens I'm not king here. Although I suppose nobody is the king at the moment, are they?"

"The Queen Melisende is a widow, milord."

"Beware the power of a political woman, Simon. I could tell you stories of my cousin Eleanor that would freeze your blood."

"St. Paul advises that women are not meant to rule over men, milord. He says that they are not temperamentally suited to it."

"Oh, that's not the problem at all," said Oliver. "The problem is that they're dangerously good at it and play the game harder than anyone."

They stopped at the entrance to a public house. A wooden sign announced that the house's patron was St. Mark, and a painting of a hanging bunch of purple grapes told passersby what they could find within.

"Seems a likely spot for gossip," said Oliver.

"Milord—"

"I won't even look at any dice," promised the English knight.

They stepped into the tavern, and Oliver looked around. It was late morning, and the company was sparse. He selected a wooden trestle table against a wall, and sat himself down, indicating to Simon to take the bench opposite him. He waited patiently for the barman to wander over.

"G'day to you, lord," said the barman, with a slight bow of his head. "How may I serve you?"

"What do you recommend?" asked Oliver, his face open and friendly. Privately, he thought the place a squalid little hole, but there was no reason to be rude.

The barman gave the trestle table a wipe down with a cloth that had seen better days. "Fresh wine to be had, lord, as well as the local ale."

"A cup of red wine for me, then, and a jack of ale for my servant," said Oliver, hoping he hadn't doomed them both to death by poison.

"M'lord," replied the barman, touching his forehead and retreating to the kitchen.

Oliver once more surveyed the company of the tavern as they waited for their drinks. The place appeared to be more of a working man's public house, and its occupants dock workers or sailors. If he had been in search of entertainment, Oliver would have looked for a better class of tavern, but in truth, he was still rattled by his almost encounter with Ruadhan that morning and had stopped in the first place that caught his eye.

The barman returned with a pewter goblet filled with wine and a boiled leather cup of ale.

"Thank you, my man," said Oliver. "I was hoping you might be able to advise me on something."

"Milord?" said the barman dubiously.

"I wish to have a little keepsake made of my journey; a palm leaf rendered in silver. Do you know of a good silversmith in the city?"

"That would be Benedetto, sir," replied the barman. "Has a stall in the market. Ask for him there, and you'll find him soon enough, sir."

"Thank you for your help," said Oliver, nodding to Simon. His servant reached into his bag and slid a silver penny across the table. The barman blinked and pushed the coin into the cloth around his waist. "Would you want any food, sir?" he asked hopefully.

Oliver suppressed a shudder and said, "No, thank you, just the drinks." The man shuffled back behind the bar.

"So," said Oliver, "Benedetto the silversmith, in the Venetian market. Worth a penny, I imagine."

"If you say so, milord," replied Simon.

"Only one problem, Simon."

"Milord?"

"I'm going to need to finish this wine before we can leave. I don't suppose you want it?"

"It says in the Proverbs, 'Wine is a mocker, strong drink is a brawler, and whoever is led astray by it is not wise,' milord."

"You know you could just say 'no,' Simon."

---

The pair left shortly afterwards, with Oliver waiting until they had travelled a block before using the water in his canteen to rinse his mouth out. "A little on the fresh side," he said, grimacing. "How was your ale?"

"Passable, milord."

"Lucky you. Does the Bible say anything about the perils of drinking ale?"

"Scripture is silent on the subject, milord," replied Simon.

"That's unusual. Scripture seems to have a lot of opinions on a lot of things. Have you ever read Leviticus, Simon?"

"Only once, milord."

"I think we turn here," said Oliver, steering them further away from the open water of the port. "I was forced to memorize the first ten chapters of Leviticus by my tutor when I was a child. Helped me learn sword fighting in those early days."

"Milord?"

"For months, years perhaps, I imagined that I was trying to kill my tutor in combat," said Oliver. "I was unstoppable. One of the best uses for the Bible I've ever found."

Simon did not reply.

The street down which they travelled opened into a square with numerous market stalls and merchants plying their trade within them. It appeared that everything from fresh produce to cloth to books was on sale in the market square, and there was a busy crowd shopping among the stalls.

"It looks like our timing could not be better," said Oliver. "It must be some sort of market day. Wait here, esteemed servant, and watch who may be watching. Hola, fellow," he said, plucking at one man's sleeve, "where might I find Benedetto the silversmith?"

He followed the man's directions and soon stood in front of a man whose wares were encased in boxes with thick glass fronts. "Greetings, noble sir," said the man, bowing slightly. He was a long, spindly creature with thinning hair mostly concealed by an extravagant blue hat. He either had not shaved that morning or was attempting to grow a beard.

"Greetings!" replied Oliver. "Might you be the man called Benedetto?"

"I have that honour, noble sir," said the merchant, bowing slightly once again. "Perhaps you have heard of my work? The finest you will find in Tyre. These pieces you see before you are but samples to whet the appetite. It is in my custom work that you will find the true genius of the Venetian technique."

"So, you are a member of the guild of silversmiths?" asked Oliver absently, looking over a case of ornate silver rings.

"I am indeed, noble sir," replied Benedetto. "The only master of the Venetian guild in Tyre."

"I am interested in commissioning a custom piece," said Oliver, looking over another case. "A friend of mine had a pendant with a magnificent silver apple." He looked up at the silversmith. "He said that a Venetian in Acre had made it, but I couldn't find the fellow. Name of Arnaldo. Is that a piece that you would be able to make?"

Benedetto's expression turned sorrowful. "Alas, noble sir, the laws of my guild prohibit me from duplicating the work of another master smith. I can produce a very beautiful apple pendant for you, but not in the same style as Arnaldo's."

"You know his style, then," pressed Oliver.

"Arnaldo di Carazzo is a skilled artist," replied Benedetto. "His style is unmistakable. He favours a very modern approach to his pieces; tries to make them more real than the thing itself. I prefer a more traditional construction. There is great merit to the classical forms. They are recognized all over the civilized world! But I am not surprised that you did not find Arnaldo in Acre."

"How do you mean?" asked Oliver, frowning.

"I know that he was planning on moving his business. Further north, I had heard? To Tripoli," said Benedetto.

"Do you happen to know why?" asked Oliver, keeping his tone casual.

"No idea." Benedetto shrugged. "Arnaldo only arrived in Outremer this year. Perhaps the city of Acre was not to his taste. It is different here compared to back home. But as to custom pieces, sir, I would be happy to sketch some potential designs for an apple pendant in my own style. I'm afraid you will have to return tomorrow afternoon; I must be here in the square for the market day."

"I am not certain," replied Oliver. "I would not wish to take up your valuable time and then not commission a piece. Perhaps I could come by your shop tomorrow. Where might I find it?"

Benedetto gave him directions, then added, "It would be a simple thing for me to sketch some designs, noble sir. I am happy to do it and have them ready for you to examine. I would not charge a fee for something so simple, and I am confident that you will find my designs to be everything you could hope for."

"You are most kind, Benedetto," said Oliver, smiling. "However, I must say that I have my heart set on the pendant my friend showed to me. Only larger, I think. I would like something more substantial. I may very well try to locate Arnaldo myself. But I must thank you for the helpful information you have provided." He discreetly placed five silver pennies next to a display case. "For your troubles."

Benedetto stared for a moment at the coins, then burst out, "There may be another way for me to help you, noble sir."

Oliver raised his eyebrows and said, "That would be very kind."

"It would be against guild law for me to duplicate the design of another master," repeated Benedetto, "but if one of my journeymen were to, for the sake of his own practice, copy another master's design as a part of his education..."

"Under the close supervision of his master," prompted Oliver.

"Precisely," agreed Benedetto. "I see that we understand each other, noble sir."

"Perhaps I could come by tomorrow and see what sketches your journeyman has come up with," Oliver said with a smile.

"It would be our honour to assist you, noble sir," replied Benedetto with a bow.

"You are too kind," Oliver said, turning to leave.

The English knight had not made it far across the square when he noticed a group of men headed determinedly his way. He deliberately did not look in the direction where he had last seen Simon. Instead, he changed his direction so that he could stand near one of the streets that led away from the square and then faced the approaching men.

"Good day, sirs," Oliver said pleasantly to the men who had gathered in a semi-circle around him. He counted five for certain. They appeared to be unarmed, but their loose-fitting clothing was capable of concealing any number of bad intentions.

"You are the Englishman, Oliver Oakeshott?" demanded the leader of the group, a heavily bearded man with missing teeth and a nose that had clearly taken too many punches. *The local head-breakers, I must assume.*

"Who might be asking?" Oliver responded, keeping his hands clear of the hilt of his sword. He would not give them the opportunity to say that he had drawn first.

"Friends of Bartolomeo de Farrugia," replied the bearded man.

"Never heard of the fellow," said Oliver instinctively. For a moment he genuinely had no idea who the man was talking about, then with a jolt remembered the Venetian merchant from Acre who carried crooked dice.

"He remembers you, Englishman," said the bearded man, smiling a gap-toothed smile. "Now come with us, and there will be no trouble."

This was an old dance, and despite Oliver's youth, it was deeply familiar to him.

"Gentlemen, I will not," he said. "My business is my own, and I have none with you." He said it loudly enough for his word to carry and hopefully be remembered by any witnesses to whatever was going to happen next. He watched the eyes of the men confronting him, who were beginning to fan out. "Good day, sirs," he said and saw the telltale flicker in the eyes of the bearded leader.

Oliver quickly pivoted, catching the arm of the sixth man behind him, who had begun to swing a heavy belaying pin directly at his head. He pulled at the man's arm until he lost balance and stumbled forward, then kneed him heavily in the face. The sound of the belaying pin clattering to the ground was loud in the silence of the square.

"May I observe that this man of yours struck first and tried to hit me from behind?" Oliver said loudly.

The bearded man scowled and shrugged. "It is no matter," he said, and pulling a short iron bar from his cloak, he charged.

For Oliver, everything extraneous disappeared as his world shrank to his immediate surroundings, and time slowed in a way it only did when he was fighting for his life. He grabbed the wrist of the bearded man and jerked him forward, lowering his own head and smashing it into the man's much-broken nose. The man howled. Oliver was already stepping into the space of another attacker, planting his knee firmly into the man's groin.

A thick club came down on his right shoulder, and even though Oliver rolled with the blow to reduce its impact, his arm went suddenly numb. The English knight continued to spin his body to add momentum to the thunderous punch he planted with his left fist into his attacker's face. The man's eyes rolled up in his head, and he went down. Oliver dipped down to grab the man's club, circling to give himself more space while he waited for the feeling in his right arm to return.

*If the shoulder is broken, I might be in trouble.*

Thankfully, he was already starting to feel a painful tingling as sensation returned. He bought himself time by stamping on the face of the man whose groin he had kneed.

*Three down for the count – ambusher, club man, bruised balls. Bearded leader struggling but conscious. Two more on their feet. Time to end it.*

He used the club to parry a blow from one of the two men left standing, then landed a vicious jab with the handle straight into the other man's midsection. As the man doubled over, air exploding from his lungs, Oliver finished him with a blow to the back of the head. He flipped the end of the club upwards to catch the final man in the chin, and as the man was falling, backhanded the bearded man in the mouth just as he was beginning to rise.

The brief demonstration of well executed brutal violence left the occupants of the market square silent and open-mouthed. Oliver bowed slightly to the crowd, said, "And a pleasant market day to you all," and took off at a run for the Templar commandery.

---

By the time Oliver reached the commandery, news of the violence had preceded him, and the forecourt was filled with Templar knights and sergeants who were spilling out from the barracks and the chapel. As they saw Oliver, men charged forward, demanding news. Some of them looked angry. He held up his hands as they surrounded him.

"Silence!" came a stern command, and the group immediately complied. The crowd parted to reveal Fabien striding forward, with Ruadhan a step behind. "Close the gates and bar them until we find out exactly what has transpired," the Templar commanded. "Oliver, Ruadhan, with me," he said, drawing them to one side.

"Heaven help us, young man, have you set the city afire?" demanded Fabien quietly and fiercely.

"I don't know, Brother," replied Oliver, leaning over with his hands on his knees to catch his breath. "I ran here as fast as I could."

"What happened?" pressed Ruadhan.

"I was making enquiries at the Venetian market when I was ambushed by a group of local bravos," said Oliver, panting.

"Are they pursuing you?" asked Fabien.

"I don't know; I was too busy running to check," said Oliver with a grin. "I don't suppose you have a drink of water handy?"

Ruadhan found him a canteen while Fabien ordered men to scout the Venetian quarter to see if further trouble was brewing.

"Oliver," whispered Ruadhan as Oliver drank gratefully, "where is Simon?"

"If we have any luck at all, he is finding out who sent those bravos after me," Oliver whispered back after wiping his mouth.

"And if we have no luck?"

"Then I'm bloody well going back there and not leaving until I find him," said Oliver grimly.

---

By the time the bell tolled for Vespers, the situation in the city had become clearer. Although badly battered, none of the attackers had died, and the ruffians were being held in cells beneath the city keep for violating the Queen's peace. Happily, the testimony of numerous witnesses confirmed that Oliver had acted only in his own defence and had never even drawn his sword. Oliver received a summons to report to the Royal

Seneschal at his convenience upon the morrow to provide his testimony.

Satisfied that the city was at peace, Fabien led the Templars into the chapel for evening prayers. Oliver, however, observed to the Knight Commander that he had a duty to inquire after his servant, who was still missing.

"Very well," said Fabien, "but we dine after Vespers, and if you miss the meal, you have only yourself to blame. Try not to set the city afire while we are at prayer," he added drily.

"Indeed, Brother. Please leave the gates open for me so that if I do need to return hastily, I can do so," replied Oliver with a cheeky grin.

The Templar regarded him for a moment and sighed. "I know who I will be praying for," he said and turned to go into the chapel.

Oliver snagged Ruadhan's sleeve. "If I do not return by Compline, look for me in the Venetian quarter."

Ruadhan nodded and clasped Oliver's arm. "I will. Be careful, for Heaven's sake."

"Pray for me," said Oliver with a twinkle in his eye, and set off.

## Chapter Ten
### RUADHAN

It was with an uncertain heart that Ruadhan turned to his prayers for the second time that day. He was having difficulty calming his spirit. Although he knew that Oliver was exceedingly capable of defending himself, Ruadhan felt like he had let the Englishman down by not being at his side when he had been attacked in the city market. Truth to tell, he also regretted having missed the fight, which sounded like a wild affair. To come out the victor against six men? City toughs rather than soldiers, but still. Ruadhan wondered if he could have done the same without drawing his sword.

"Come, let us sing to the Lord and shout with joy to the Rock who saves us," intoned Fabien. "Let us approach him with praise and thanksgiving and sing joyful songs to the Lord."

Ruadhan and the other Templars recited the antiphon together: "Come, let us worship before the Lord, our maker."

Fabien continued. "The Lord is God, the mighty God, the great king over all the gods. He holds in his hands the depths of the earth and the highest mountains as well. He made the sea; it belongs to him, the dry land, too, for it was formed by his hands."

"Come, let us worship before the Lord, our maker," the assembly responded.

Ruadhan let the words of the evening prayer wash over him as he fell into its familiar rhythms. There was a great peace to be found in the concept of surrender to a higher power. *Whatever this mystery we follow may be, if it is God's will that we uncover it, we shall.* Thoughts of their mission led the Irish knight straight towards thoughts of Oliver. *God, is it so wrong to love?* The idea felt painful. Truth to tell, his heart ached thinking about Oliver. The man was so beautiful, so filled with life, bursting with energy and humour, blessed with prodigious strength and skill. In Oliver Oakeshott, God had created a man that celebrated the joy of living in everything he did.

"Your will be done, O Lord," murmured Ruadhan, once again attempting to put his future in God's hands. "If this is meant to be, nothing will oppose it. If it is not Your will, there is nothing I can do to make it happen."

As Vespers ended, the Templars raised themselves from their knees and proceeded to the refectory for their evening meal. Ruadhan, more at peace with himself than he had been for some time, joined the line of knights leaving the chapel.

The evening meal was a quiet affair, as the knights were obliged by their Rule to eat in silence. Long ago, Ruadhan had learned the series of hand signals by which food and drink were passed along the table without the need for words. This allowed the community to listen to the words of the lector, a specially designated reader who would read from scripture while the Templars ate.

The evening's reading was from Second Samuel; the story

of how King David seduced Bathsheba, the wife of Uriah the Hittite. Ruadhan raised an eyebrow as he silently chewed his food. This was heady stuff for a community of celibate men, and he had served in commanderies where these passages were conveniently omitted, with Knight Commanders deciding that the faithful knights did not need to hear stories about spying on naked women in their baths. Unfortunately for Ruadhan's peace of mind, the passage reminded him of the steam bath he and Oliver had taken earlier that day.

When he had travelled to Outremer, Ruadhan and his fellow novice Templars had stopped briefly in Constantinople, taking in the sights of the legendary city. Ruadhan had seen ancient Greek statues in which the powerful forms of naked and near-naked men had been lovingly sculpted. What Ruadhan had seen of Oliver's nude form could have given any of those statues a run for their money. The Englishman was powerfully built and made for war; every part of his muscular body was like a work of art.

The Irishman took a deep breath, and silently gestured for the jug of water he shared with his tablemates. He shifted slightly and was grateful for the concealing nature of the table. Desire was a hard serpent to wrestle with.

As if summoned by Ruadhan's thoughts, Oliver appeared at the entrance to the refectory, scanning the room, made eye contact with Ruadhan and gave him a small nod.

*He must have found Simon*, thought the Irishman, relieved.

The English knight took a free spot at another table in silence and proceeded to demolish a substantial joint of beef, washing it down with wine. His tablemates glanced at each other with expressions of amusement, but Oliver did not seem to notice them, intent as he was on eating as if this was his last meal.

Ruadhan was too excited to have much more appetite and waited impatiently for his brethren to finish their meal and for the lector to finish his reading. Finally, the lector closed his Bible and turned to a smaller book, reading out a portion of the Rule of the Templar Order:

"Rule Fifteen. Although the reward of poverty, which is the kingdom of heaven, is without a doubt reserved for the poor in spirit, nevertheless, we bid you, whom the Christian faith unquestionably exhorts concerning them, to give daily as your alms a tenth of your bread."

*I think Oliver just ate it,* thought Ruadhan, and had to stifle his laughter. The lector closed the copy of the Rule, and the Templars stood up from their benches and walked from the room. Ruadhan followed Oliver out to the forecourt, where they found Simon waiting.

The Irish Templar clasped the servant's arms. "It cheers my heart to see you well," he said with feeling. In truth, he had grown very fond of the man, and the relief he felt at seeing him again surprised him.

"Thank you, milord. I am glad to be well and to be able to see you again," said Simon.

"I found him on his way to return here," said Oliver proudly. "He did not need my help at all and has done clever work today! Tell Ruadhan what you told me," he prompted.

"Thank you, milord," said Simon. "While my lord Oliver spoke with the silversmith, I watched the crowd. I believed that I saw one man observing my lord very closely, and as I watched, the fellow left the square, returning later with the five ruffians who threatened my lord. Confident that Sir Oliver did not need my help, I followed the man instead, who left quite quickly as the confrontation began. The fellow led me on a merry chase, my lords, and I was hard put to avoid being found out. Finally, he went to ground in a house on the northern side of the city. I stayed to observe him, lords, until I could be certain that he remained there. I have held my watch for the past hour or more and was on my way back here when I encountered my lord Oliver in the street."

"Did I not say he has done clever work today?" said Oliver. "I knew you would want to join me, so I came to collect you, and the meat smelled so delicious that I thought it would do no harm for me to replenish my spirits while I waited for you to finish your meal." A thought struck him. "Simon, have you eaten since we returned?"

"There was still some porridge in the servants' quarters, milord."

Oliver made a face. "Cold?"

"Cold, milord," replied Simon.

"So much for 'the last shall be first,'" said Oliver ruefully. "But apparently the Templar knights give away a tenth of their food, so there is that. It was beef, and it was delicious. But not until later this evening, Simon! We must be upon our evening's hunt before the quarry hides away."

"I will need to tell Brother Fabien," said Ruadhan. "He may even give us some reinforcements."

"Then go, but quickly!" said Oliver, who was almost vibrating with excitement. "I hate to think of this fellow slipping off into the night."

"You made time enough to fill your belly," observed Ruadhan, laughing as he strode towards the Knight Commander's chambers.

"I was hungry!" Oliver called back plaintively.

---

Fabien did indeed give them reinforcements: five tough Templar sergeants who looked capable of handling themselves. The whole group went armed but forsook armour as the enemy of quiet movement. Soon the group was threading its way through the streets of Tyre, moving quickly so as to forestall any opportunity for warning. It was the twilit time between Vespers and Compline; the sun had fallen below the horizon, but full night had not yet claimed the city. There were few people on the streets, and those that were there were hurrying home for their own evening meals. The air in the city was smoky as people lit the hearth fires in their homes.

"The next block, milords; left at the corner up ahead," said Simon quietly. Ruadhan held up his hand to signal the men to halt, then drew them close.

"Do you know the street up ahead?" he asked, and the sergeants nodded. "Good. You four, go one street down until you are near the back of the house. Seize anyone who attempts to run. You, come with Sir Oliver and me. We will break down the front door. Remember, we are here to capture, not to kill. Deaths will not serve us here. Now go, and God be with you!"

The four sergeants loped off into the evening. Ruadhan silently counted to sixty in his head, then nodded to the others. "Let's go," he said.

A woman walking down the street eyed them suspiciously before clasping her basket more closely and hurrying along.

The dusk deepened as they turned the corner and approached the house that Simon indicated. It was a squat mud brick construction with deep slits for windows. From the flickering light within, it appeared that a fire was burning. The sounds of a rebab floated mournfully into the evening.

"What's that?" whispered Oliver. "It sounds like someone's torturing a tuned cat. And what's that smell?"

Ruadhan chuckled softly. "It's a local musical instrument. And the smell is odd. Like cooking spices, but not quite."

"Tough looking door," murmured Oliver dourly. "Iron hinges."

"Hmm. You're right." Ruadhan scanned up and down the street, looking for anything that might serve as a battering ram, but there were no likely candidates. He turned to the remaining Templar sergeant. "How heavy is that axe?" he asked.

The man grinned. "Lead weighted, Brother. It's meant to be an armour-breaker."

"Good man. When it's time, set to that door with a will," said Ruadhan.

"Yes, Brother."

"Simon, stay behind us," said Oliver, drawing a short blade.

"Yes, milord."

Ruadhan drew his knife – a sword would be useless in the confines of the house – and looked at the others. They looked back at him. "Let's go," he said, and the four men rushed across the street.

"Go for the hinges," hissed Ruadhan to the sergeant, who, with a running start, took a massive swing at the top section of the door. His axe bit deeply into the wood, and the door shuddered.

The rebab music from inside abruptly halted, and Ruadhan heard a man curse. The Templar sergeant took a second swing, this time at the lower hinge. There was a hissing sound within, and foul-smelling smoke rolled out of the deep-set window closest to the door.

The sergeant swung again at the top hinge, which was badly bent, and it gave way with a sound of tortured metal. Oliver shoved heavily at the door and cursed. "Barred," he said, rubbing his shoulder.

"Again!" Ruadhan shouted to the Templar sergeant, inwardly cursing at the time this was taking. The man grunted and gave another heavy swing at the lower hinge, crushing it beyond recognition. The door was now mangled everywhere except the middle, where a bar held it firm. Ruadhan stepped forward and seized the door's upper half, pulling on it with all his strength. The splintered wood groaned and gave way, spilling Ruadhan onto his back. Oliver kicked savagely at the bottom section, which fell away until only the bar remained in the middle of the doorframe. A cloud of smoke billowed out from the interior.

Ruadhan had already regained his footing and rolled under the bar, cursing as he tried to see through the thick smoke. He coughed as he stood and lifted the bar from its bracket. Oliver followed him inside and waved at the coiling smoke.

As best as the Irish knight could tell, there was no one in the front room. A brazier filled with coals had been knocked over, and he stamped on them with his boot.

"There's no one here!" he shouted, coughing again as the smoke filled his lungs. "Check the other rooms. When you find the back door, open it and let the others in!"

The house had but one level and four rooms, and soon they had the back door open and a welcome cross breeze blowing the smoke away. Of the house's inhabitant, however, there was no sign.

"Check the roof," ordered Ruadhan, trying to stifle his insistent cough. Two Templar sergeants hurried to obey. "Dammit, Oliver, where has he gone?"

Oliver's eyes were red from the smoke. "He can't have disappeared. There must be something we're missing."

"Milords!" called Simon from the front room, and they rushed to join him. Oliver's servant had peeled back a section of the thick rug that covered the floor, revealing a wooden trapdoor.

"A tunnel!" Oliver cursed, coughing. "Well done, Simon." He pulled at the trapdoor handle , but it would not budge. "Bolted again," he said. "I'm beginning to dislike this fellow. Sergeant, I have a job for you!" he called, directing the axe-wielding Templar to the trapdoor. "Ruadhan, we'll need torches if we're going down there," he said.

"More bloody smoke," said Ruadhan. His head felt thick, and the thuds of the axe were loud in his ears. "Who has the torches?" he called, and another of the sergeants stepped forward with two wooden staves, each of them with an end wrapped in thick cloth soaked in pitch. "Good man," said Ruadhan. "Light them, will you?"

By this time the Templar axeman had finished demolishing the trapdoor, and Oliver was peering inside. He swayed slightly as he leaned over. "Blessed Mary, it feels like my lungs have been scoured with wire," he grumbled. "A torch here when they're ready," said Oliver, reaching out his hand. A sergeant passed him a lit torch, and Oliver dipped it down into the hole. "There are steps cut into the side," he said. "Goes down maybe ten, twelve feet, then it turns."

"Right," said Ruadhan grimly. "Sir Oliver and I will go down. You, the handy fellow with the axe. What's your name?"

"Gregory, Brother."

"Gregory, you come with us. There may be more doors in our future. The rest of you, stay here and make sure no one comes down this tunnel after us. Simon, go back to the commandery and tell Brother Fabien what has happened, and ask him to send more men."

"That's my servant," said Oliver admonishingly, "you can't tell him what to do."

Ruadhan simply looked at the English knight.

"Simon, go back to the commandery and tell Brother Fabien what has happened, and ask him to send more men," said Oliver.

"Milord," replied Simon with a nod, and went to do his duty.

"Right," said Ruadhan. "Gregory, you go down first; there may be other barriers. I'll go next. Oliver, you follow at the rear."

"Whatever your heart desires," said Oliver. Ruadhan looked at him again.

"Oliver, are you well?" he asked.

"Sorry," said Oliver, shaking his head. "Don't know why I said that. Carry on."

Ruadhan frowned at him, then gestured at the Templar sergeant to start going down the stairs. Gregory slipped down to the bottom of the steps, then held up his torch and peered down the tunnel. He looked up.

"It's narrow, Brother," he said. "No more than one may fit at a time. I can't see the end."

"I'm coming," replied Ruadhan, descending the steps. He looked past Gregory's shoulder. The tunnel was narrow, hewn from dirt with wooden braces. It felt menacing in a way Ruadhan was unable to articulate.

"Coming down," said Oliver from above.

"Let's go," said Ruadhan, putting his hand on Gregory's shoulder.

Cautiously, they made their way down the tunnel. It was slightly lower than the average man's height, so they had to crouch. The burning torches made the air hot, and everything felt very close. Ruadhan tried not to think of the weight of the earth just above their heads or the possibility that the tunnel could collapse and bury them all.

The tunnel turned to the right, and as they followed the turn, Gregory suddenly shouted, "Merciful God!"

In sheer terror, the Templar sergeant turned and tried to run past Ruadhan, cursing and swearing. Ruadhan struggled to keep his feet as the sturdy man clutched at him. Oliver shouted behind him, demanding to know what was going on. Gregory, thoroughly terrified, finally managed to shove past Ruadhan, who dropped his torch onto the tunnel floor. As the sergeant bowled into Oliver, the English knight shouted once more in frustration and gave Gregory a punch to the side of the head that felled the Templar sergeant like a stunned ox.

Ruadhan, in the meantime, regained his feet and picked up his torch. He still had no idea what had panicked Gregory, and his heart was pounding. What lay around the corner?

"What in the name of Heaven is happening?" demanded Oliver.

Ruadhan poked his head around the corner and was greeted with a vision from Hell.

Around the corner was a gateway of yellowed bone, and the bones had been taken from no man or beast that Ruadhan had ever seen or heard of, with strange spikes and malformed humps, yet somehow bound together seamlessly. From the top of the gateway hung a hideous mass of snakes, their tails curved around the bony gateway, their bodies writhing sinuously as they hissed at Ruadhan and darted at his face, their fangs dripping with venom.

"Christ, protect me!" he shouted, falling backwards in horror, scrabbling at the tunnel floor to get back around the corner.

"Ruadhan, what's going on?" shouted Oliver once more, dragging his friend backwards and stepping over him to peer around the corner.

"Oliver, for God's love, be careful!" begged Ruadhan, grabbing at his heel.

Oliver turned the corner and lifted his torch. "What is it?" he demanded. "There's nothing here. Is there something past the beads?"

"Beads?" cried Ruadhan. "Look out for the serpents, man!"

Oliver looked at him and frowned. "Serpents?" he said, then took another step around the turn. "Ruadhan, there's nothing here. Just a beaded archway, then more tunnel. I think I can see a ladder in the distance."

"What?" Ruadhan struggled to his feet and tried to slow his breathing down. His heart was racing. "Where did the snakes go?" He took a deep breath and turned the corridor.

Oliver was right. Just around the corner was a wood archway set into the tunnel, featuring a number of strings of green glass beads. He ran his hand over them, felt them pass through his fingers. "They *are* beads. Oliver, what did I just see? And why did Gregory see it, too?"

"I think I know," said Oliver grimly. "Stay here, and look to

Gregory, make sure he's still breathing. I won't be but a moment."

Ruadhan fiercely quelled his rising panic at the thought of being alone in the tunnel with an unconscious Gregory and nodded. "I'll be back," said Oliver, proceeding down the tunnel. Ruadhan waited, focusing on his breathing, and moments later Oliver returned. There was a gust of fresh air through the tunnel, and the beads trembled on their strings.

"The tunnel opens just outside the city walls," said Oliver. "No one there. Just a moonlit night. Come on, let's get back to the others, and bring Gregory back to the surface. Our quarry is gone."

"Oliver, what in Heaven's name just happened? I don't understand," pleaded Ruadhan.

"There is nothing to fear, Ruadhan. I'll tell you all once we are out of the tunnel and breathing fresh air."

---

With some help from the other Templar sergeants, they lifted Gregory's unconscious body out of the tunnel and set him down on the floor of the front room. "Take him outside and lay him in the street," ordered Oliver once he had climbed out of the tunnel. "We're all going out into the street. We need fresh air; I'll explain."

Eventually, the entire group assembled out front of their target house. Moments later, Simon arrived, rushing down the street with a collection of Templar knights and sergeants in tow.

"Milord?" asked Simon, running towards his master.

"Fear not, Simon; all is well," said Oliver tiredly. "We are not in any danger. I'm afraid we lost the man you followed, though; I am sorry." He looked around at the gathering of men. "If you please, I would recommend setting a watch on this house. Do not go in, however, or allow anyone else to go in. The house is dangerous, but it should be harmless in a few hours or so."

"Oliver, can you please tell us what is going on?" asked Ruadhan.

"I'd rather wait until we are with Brother Fabien," replied Oliver. "But I can tell you now that although we are going to be alright, we have been poisoned."

---

"Poisoned?" asked Fabien, an expression of concern on his face. At Oliver's suggestion, he had provided plenty of drinking water and foodstuffs. Ruadhan was grateful; for some reason, he was absolutely starving.

"It took me forever to recognize," replied Oliver, shaking his head. "When I was in Constantinople, I once found myself in a rather disreputable place that offered a variety of services. Unfortunately, I was caught up in certain things before I was able to disentangle myself."

*I'll bet you were*, thought Ruadhan, but kept the thought to himself.

"Several patrons of this establishment were smoking pipes which emitted the most malodorous smoke," continued Oliver. "I caught a great deal of it in my lungs. It left me with the most pleasant sensations at first, but then things sort of turned – I saw things that were impossible to reckon with as a part of this world. I saw what I thought were visions of Heaven and Hell."

"Like what I saw when we turned the corner!" cried

Ruadhan in realization. "Blessed Mary, the smoke! We all breathed the heavy smoke that filled the house. Do you mean we're all poisoned?"

"The effects fade," said Oliver, lifting a placatory hand. "I imagine we are through all but the smallest lingering effects."

"So, what is this substance?" asked Fabien, frowning.

"In Constantinople, they called it *hashish*," replied Oliver.

"This is what I was afraid of," said Fabien grimly. "Both of you have heard of the Assassins, of course."

Ruadhan felt understanding begin to dawn, but Oliver looked puzzled.

Fabien continued. "The word 'assassin' is a corruption of the original Arabic, which is *hashshashin*, which means 'hashish eaters.'"

"Wait," said Oliver, shaking his head.

"Of course, some scholars say the word is *hashshishiyyun*, or even *asasiyyun*," Fabien continued, "but as your experience tonight can attest to –"

"Brother," interjected Oliver, "are you telling me that tonight we pursued an Assassin? And that he escaped through a tunnel underneath the city wall?"

Fabien looked surprised at being interrupted. "Yes, I would say that seems to be the case."

Oliver looked at Ruadhan. "And I would say that our quest for Peter Thistle has taken a turn."

"It certainly casts a different light on the murder of the Venetian silversmith," replied Ruadhan. His mind was racing. "We may have to rethink a lot of things."

"Well, it is now confirmed," announced Oliver, "I can now say with confidence that I no longer have any idea what is going on." He turned to Fabien. "I don't suppose you have anything stronger than water to hand?"

## Chapter Eleven
### OLIVER

Happily, Oliver had been able to sleep through Matins without so much as rolling over, but they rang the bells for Prime; indeed, bells rang throughout the city to announce the breaking of dawn. Over the years, Oliver had learned to ignore the ringing of Prime as part of the price to be paid for city life, but the Templar chapel was quite close to the guest house, and so it felt to Oliver as if someone was ringing the bell right next to his bedside.

"No help for it," he said to himself with a groan and hauled himself out of bed.

During his morning ablutions, he considered what they had learned the night before.

*Assassins? It's like something out of a story.*

Ruadhan seemed to take their presence much more in stride, but in fairness, the Templar had been here for longer, and the deadly killers' presence here in Outremer was much less exotic and more a part of the risks of life on the frontiers of Christianity.

He opened the door of his chamber to call for Simon, who was walking down the hallway towards him.

"Milord?" asked Simon.

"Your timing, dear servant, is as impeccable as always," said Oliver, feeling strangely reassured by Simon's familiar presence. The events of the previous night and their implications had been jarring, and Oliver was glad for the constancy that Simon represented.

"Thank you, milord. What might you require this morning, milord?"

"Breakfast," said Oliver firmly. "When everything has been turned on its head, there's nothing like a good breakfast to set things right. Are we supposed to dine with the Templars, or can we just go ahead and eat? I'm ravenous."

"The brothers are still at Prime prayers, milord. I will see what there is to be had in the kitchen and bring you up a tray," said Simon.

Oliver expressed his gratitude and set to the task of shaving. He was still young enough that he did not have to do so every day, but they had been some time in the wilderness, and he thought he was beginning to look a little scraggly. Simon arrived just as he was finishing.

"Good man," said Oliver. "How much longer will our hosts be praying?"

"I'm not certain, milord."

"Seems like a lot of prayer for fighting men," said Oliver, taking a bite out of a fresh apple. "By Heaven, that's delicious."

"Perhaps, milord, they feel that fighting men have a lot to pray about," said Simon.

"I suppose so," said Oliver doubtfully. "Do have a bite of this apple, Simon; it's absolutely heavenly. But wasn't that part of the promise of the pilgrimage to the Holy Land? Die fighting the infidel, and you're a martyr who pops straight up to Heaven and all that?"

"I do not know the technicalities, milord," replied Simon as he chewed thoughtfully.

"Isn't it divine?" asked Oliver, referring to the apple. "Anyway, it does seem odd. If anyone has high odds of dying while fighting the infidel, it would be a Templar. All these extra prayers seem a bit unnecessary."

"I think," said Simon, "that the prayers reinforce their calling, milord."

Oliver looked up. "Well, it seems that they are over for the moment, thank goodness." Outside the window of his chambers in the guesthouse, a line of knights was proceeding from the chapel to the refectory. "I'll see if I can't grab a little more to eat while they have their meal. See about getting yourself something, Simon; you must be positively fading away."

"Yes, milord."

---

After the morning meal, Oliver met with Ruadhan and Fabien in the Knight Commander's chamber. Fabien took a rolled parchment from a shelf and spread it on the table, weighing it down with a heavy inkwell and some books.

"What are we looking at here, Brother?" asked Oliver.

"Central Outremer," replied Fabien. "The northern reaches of the Kingdom as well as the County of Tripoli."

Oliver nodded. "*Why* are we looking at this, Brother?"

"Because of the involvement of the Assassins," Ruadhan

interjected. "Last night's discoveries have certain, well, implications."

"Did you two consult with each other during your morning prayers?" asked Oliver. "Because I'm feeling a bit left out in the cold here."

"Forgive us," said Ruadhan, "we do not mean to talk in riddles. Brother Fabien, if I may?"

Fabien waved a hand for him to continue.

"There are many different kinds of people that live in Outremer, as we talked about before," said Ruadhan. "Including many different kinds of Saracens. Probably the strangest are the Assassins. They claim to worship the Saracen god, but the other Saracens hate them and often drive them out when they are discovered. So, the Assassins worship secretly, except in a few remote places in the distant mountains where they have castles and can live and pray without fear of persecution."

"I have heard of so-called Christians in southern France who do the same," Oliver observed.

"Even so," replied Ruadhan. "But what makes the Assassins different, and particularly dangerous, is their willingness to use murder as a political tool."

"Doesn't sound all that unusual," Oliver snorted. "How is that different from what the pilgrim fighters did in Jerusalem all those years ago? They slaughtered a city to claim it for God."

Fabien raised his eyebrows.

"I should have spoken more precisely," said Ruadhan patiently. "The difference, you could argue, is in the lengths that the Assassins are willing to go in order to accomplish their goals. Their members will spend years infiltrating the ranks of a palace guard or a noble's retinue to accomplish their mission, then when ordered, strike at their target with no regard for their own safety."

"This is why they are terrifying," interjected Fabien. "How can you protect yourself against someone who does not care if they escape? Whom you may have known for years?"

Oliver sat back, astounded. "And all of these Assassins are willing to lay down their lives in a heartbeat at the orders of their superiors? Even after having served other masters for months or years?" He shook his head. "The dedication you would need, the trust in your subordinates to obey your commands..."

"You begin to see why everyone fears them," said Fabien. "Christian and Saracen alike."

"I find it hard to understand why they have not simply been wiped out," said Oliver. "Who would tolerate such a nest of serpents on their doorstep?"

"A fair question," replied Ruadhan, "but the answer is not so simple. For one thing, no one knows the full extent of their network. They operate in secret throughout Outremer and the Saracen territories. The only place where they live openly is practically inaccessible. In addition, who would want to be the person who declared war on the Assassins? Your life would be measured in days."

"So, these people operate completely outside of anyone's control?" asked Oliver in disbelief.

"Almost completely," said Ruadhan. "The only ones who exact anything from them are, well, us."

"The Order of the Temple and the Order of the Hospital," Fabien clarified. "The Assassins pay us a certain amount in silver coin every year as tribute."

"Alright," said Oliver, "now you've lost me completely. They pay you money? Why?"

"Look at the map," Fabien instructed, and Oliver did so. In one corner of the map, he could see territories marked as belonging to the Assassins. There were several castles, villages, and towns. In every direction outside of Assassin territory was a castle marked as belonging to the Templars or the Hospitallers.

"You have them surrounded," observed Oliver.

"We do," agreed Fabien with a nod. "The Assassins pay us a silver tribute every year to allow their goods to flow freely through the passes."

Oliver frowned. "Why do they not threaten the Orders with murder in the same manner they do with everyone else?"

"They tried to, at first," said Ruadhan. "But the Orders are not like noble families. If the head of a commandery is murdered, someone else is always ready to take their place. That is true all the way up to the Grand Masters of the Orders. The Assassins could kill any one of us, but not all of us, and whoever remained would seal the passes and make their lives impossible. The Orders might even be provoked to fully commit to the bloody business of conquering Assassin territory."

"Thus, they take the path of least resistance and pay us tribute," said Fabien. "They complain but dare do nothing more, and the nobles of Outremer pay us for keeping a watch on the feared Assassins."

Oliver shook his head as he considered this information. It was a neat little arrangement, at least as far as the military Orders were concerned. "All right," he said, "I now consider myself to be well educated on the nature of the Assassins, although I will tell you frankly that I find all of this very challenging to believe. So how does this affect what we have been assigned to do?"

"A fair question," said Ruadhan. "Here's what I'm thinking, and I will admit that this is only a thread. Follow along with me and see if it makes sense to you. So, obviously, the fellow who eluded us last night was an Assassin, and he was the one who tried to get you killed in the Venetian market. Why would he do that? Not just for the mischief of it; that's not how these people do things."

Oliver nodded. "Following so far," he said.

"So, the only reason the Assassin would have had to set those ruffians on you would be to get rid of you for some reason. And the only thing that you were doing that needed stopping was..."

"...pursuing Peter Thistle," finished Oliver. He sat up. "Do you think that Peter Thistle is a member of the Assassins?"

"That's the conclusion I'm coming to," said Ruadhan, and Fabien nodded in agreement. "For some reason, an Assassin was traveling with the pilgrim caravan. He must have had something to do with Arnaldo's death. And when you went looking for him, he's probably the one who knocked you unconscious and fled."

"But it wasn't the same man here in Tyre, was it?" pressed Oliver. "I mean, was it Peter Thistle – or whatever his real name is – who set those ruffians onto me?"

"It could have been," replied Ruadhan. "Simon never saw him in the pilgrim caravan, so he would have no way of recognizing him. But whether it was him or not, he's certainly gone now; so the question is, what is our next step?"

"I have some thoughts on that," observed Fabien. "I would suggest that you need some more information on what exactly the Assassins are up to. For that, you need expertise, and that means going either north or south."

"Go on," said Oliver.

"To the north are the Banu Munqidh, a powerful Saracen family whose feud with the Assassins runs deep. The family has often been a friend to our Order and are very well informed on the doings of their hated enemies," said Fabien.

"And to the south?" asked Ruadhan.

"The council of those Templars who are most directly involved in the yearly negotiations over tribute with the Assassins. The council is headed by a brother named Gautier de Mesnil," replied Fabien.

Ruadhan and Oliver looked at each other and said at the same time, "We go north."

---

They waited until the high heat of the day had subsided, and the three men were on their way. Fabien had helpfully loaned them a pack horse and filled that horse's saddlebags with a plentiful amount of food and water. Ruadhan and Oliver opted to leave one of their spare mounts at the commandery so that they continued to travel with five horses. They needed to travel quickly and could not afford to lose time to a lame horse.

"Going north along the coast will be your best option," Fabien had told them, tracing a route along the map. "Up the Ladder of Tyre to Tripoli, and then inland towards Shaizar, the home of the Banu Munqidh."

"At least we're getting away from the desert," observed Oliver as they rode out of the city and took the northern road.

"The Kingdom has some rough and barren lands, to be

sure," said Ruadhan, "but what you have seen is nothing compared to the far south and the desert of the Empty Quarter. A man can perish in less than a day."

"How charming," groaned Oliver, "remind me to never visit there."

In truth, Oliver was getting a real education in the nature of the lands of Outremer. As Ruadhan had commented upon before, the English knight had never left the city of Acre. Now, he had trekked with a pilgrim caravan through the wastelands, seen the beauty of Tyre, nearly been killed at least twice, and now was proceeding along the beautiful Mediterranean coastline of the northern Kingdom. It really had been a remarkable adventure since he and Simon had been forced to leave Acre.

Meeting Ruadhan was at the absolute forefront of those experiences. He was a beautiful man; Oliver thought he looked like a stern angel, although he also loved those moments when the sternness left his face to be replaced by light and laughter. Ruadhan was long-limbed, taller than Oliver, and with strength and breadth in his chest and shoulders. Then, there was his skill as a warrior, which Oliver found enthralling.

All of that taken together might have led to Oliver having an infatuation with the Irish knight; but as the days had gone by and the two of them had gotten to know each other better, those feelings had deepened. Oliver had learned that Ruadhan viewed the world very differently than he did, although Oliver did not find their views mutually exclusive. In truth, Oliver envied Ruadhan his sense of wonder at the world, his excitement at the nature of God's creations, and what was at heart a mindset that was simply more open to possibilities. Oliver tended to be more cynical and hard-bitten, and he wondered if there were things he had been missing because of an attitude that had grown world-weary.

Then, there had been those moments in the steam bath. *God!* Oliver was left to only wonder what might have happened if they had not been interrupted. Certainly, he knew that he had been ready for anything and everything. He wondered if the same had been true for Ruadhan. He would have given a great deal to know for certain.

"Look at that," said Ruadhan, breaking Oliver out of his reverie. He followed to where Ruadhan was pointing and saw a ship just offshore making heavy going in the water.

"What's the fellow doing?" frowned Oliver, watching the ship struggle. It was a small vessel with a crew of no more than five, and it seemed to be caught between a high wind offshore and a strong tide. The winds were driving the ship away from shore, but the tide pulled it back, making it look like the ship was stuck in place.

"If that wind shifts, that ship will be pulled right onto the rocks," said Ruadhan. "Come on; we can't just sit and watch." He spurred his horse and rode for the beach.

"What in God's name are we supposed to do about it?" Oliver cried, but spurred his horse nevertheless. "Come on, Simon!" he called.

Ruadhan was already on the beach and off his horse, tying a length of rope to the pommel of his saddle by the time Oliver caught up with him. "Planning on steering the ship with a horse, are we?" Oliver asked sarcastically.

"Can you swim?" asked Ruadhan, ignoring Oliver's question. "Here, do what I'm doing," he continued, handing Oliver another length of rope.

"I know enough not to drown," replied Oliver dubiously,

tying the end of a rope to the pommel of his saddle. "Ruadhan, what exactly *are* we doing?"

By this point, Ruadhan was stripping down to his smallclothes. "I grew up near a wrecker's coast," he said. "Ships who didn't know the area would sometimes get pulled onto the rocks. We rescued their crews when we could." He looked up at the sky and sniffed. "Damn. Wind is shifting already. Come on, we need to get out into the water."

"And do what?" cried Oliver, who had likewise stripped down. Ruadhan tied the other end of his length of rope around his waist and did the same for Oliver. "Simon, when you see one of us wave, lead the horses to pull us back to shore."

"He's my servant," Oliver muttered, but Ruadhan had already run to the water and dived into a wave. "Don't let us die, please," he called to Simon as he began his jog to the waterline.

"Yes, milord!" he heard Simon call back.

The water was not as cold as Oliver had feared; in fact, it was rather refreshing. He spluttered as a wave took him unaware, then his instincts took over, and he began to swim powerfully out to where he saw Ruadhan. The rope was an uncomfortable weight around his waist, but he kicked forward and finally caught up to the Irish knight.

Oliver flipped his hair back from his face. "They might not even –" he began when a huge cracking, snapping sound split the air. As the wind had shifted, the tide had pulled the ship onto an outcropping of rocks offshore, and the hull had broken. The ship had already rolled on its side, and they could hear the cries of the men onboard.

"To us!" shouted Ruadhan. "To us! We'll pull you to shore!" Oliver saw that one man had jumped from the side of the ship onto the rocks and was now pointing at Ruadhan and Oliver.

"Yes! Yes!" cried Ruadhan. "To us! The tide will wash you from the rocks! Come now!"

The man had been joined by another sailor, and they seemed to be talking. Finally, the first man grabbed the second one by the sleeve and they both jumped into the water.

"Come on now, Oliver!" demanded Ruadhan, who began to swim towards the two men. The ship made a horrible noise like a moan, followed by a series of explosive cracks, and shifted further. The two men apparently knew how to swim and closed the distance.

"Good man," said Oliver, grabbing one fellow under his arm, "I've got you." With his other arm, he tried to wave as best he could. "Now, Simon! Now!" he shouted. On the shore, he could see Simon start to lead the horses up the beach.

"You'll be alright," Oliver heard Ruadhan saying to the second man, whom the Irish knight held. The man cried out something, but it came out more as a strangled gargle. Then Oliver felt the pull at his waist, and he was able to focus on keeping his man's head out of the water as the horse pulled him quickly through the water and back to shore.

Once they were clear of the waves, Oliver let the man go and collapsed on his back on the sand. "Woooo," he said, "I can't believe that worked." Ruadhan was already standing over him, pulling him to his feet. "Come on, Oliver," he urged, "there are others still out there."

"You can't be serious," Oliver protested, but Ruadhan was already running towards the water. "I'm starting to dislike you!" he shouted, setting his shoulders and running after him.

The outward swim was much worse than the swim back, in part because of Oliver's tiredness but mostly because he had to fight the tide once more. This time, it was much more challenging to swim past the breakers and fight the waves trying to drive him back to shore. The rope around his waist felt like an anchor, and despite all his efforts, he did not seem to be making it any closer to the rocks where the ship lay broken.

Oliver shouted in frustration and drove his limbs through the water, making progress through a combination of anger and sheer force of will. Finally, he reached where Ruadhan was treading water and intermittently pushed himself higher out of the water to see farther.

"They're gone!" shouted Oliver. "Ruadhan, they're all gone!"

"They can't be!" cried Ruadhan fiercely. "There must be more!"

Just then, as the noises from the ship paused briefly, they heard a thin and reedy cry from the direction of the rocks.

"There!" said Ruadhan and began to swim toward the direction of the noise.

Oliver followed suit, but he could not match Ruadhan's speed. His limbs felt heavy. He watched as Ruadhan pulled himself out of the water and onto the rocks. He saw Ruadhan lift what appeared to be a small child's body. The Irish knight waved frantically toward the shore, then jumped back into the water with the child.

As Oliver swam up to Ruadhan, he saw a boy in his arms. "Hold onto me," Ruadhan gasped, "and I will keep the child above water. Holy Mary, Oliver, keep me up; I'm just about done."

Oliver wrapped his arms around Ruadhan's chest, just under the Templar's armpits. He held onto him fiercely, striving to keep his friend's head above the water without submerging himself. Oliver could feel Ruadhan's chest expanding and contracting against him as the Irishman struggled to keep his breathing even. Oliver kicked his legs to add to the speed with which their ropes pulled them home.

"I've got you," Oliver gasped into Ruadhan's ear, "I've got you. I'm not letting you go."

A wave unexpectedly caught Oliver, and he coughed as he fought to drive the seawater from his lungs. "Don't let go!" shouted Ruadhan, craning his head back. "We're almost there!" The child in Ruadhan's arms was also coughing and beginning to thrash about frantically. "Be still, boy!" cried Ruadhan. "We're saving you! You'll be on shore soon."

Finally, they could feel sand beneath their feet. The horses still pulled, however, and they fought to keep their balance. "Simon, enough!" shouted Oliver as the horses gave a mighty tug, and Ruadhan, Oliver, and the boy all ended up in a heap on the wet sand. Oliver rolled onto his back and focused on his lungs, pushing his body to take in more air.

"That might," he panted, "be the hardest thing I've ever done." He opened his eyes and looked up. A fierce-looking group of men surrounded him, Ruadhan and the boy, all armed with spears pointing downwards at the trio.

"Huh!" exclaimed Oliver tiredly. "Where were you lot twenty minutes ago, when we could have used you?"

## Chapter Twelve
### RUADHAN

Ruadhan did not move as he looked at the spearmen warily. He counted ten men that he could see and judged by their attire that they were Arabs and probably part of a noble's retinue.

None of the men said a word, and their leaf-bladed spears did not move.

The boy lying next to Ruadhan began to cough, and Ruadhan slowly moved to sit up and rub the boy's back. The child shuddered, gave an enormous belch, and vomited up about a cupful of seawater.

There was the sound of running feet on the sand, and the spearmen parted to let a man in richly embroidered robes through. He gave a cry at the sight of the boy and swept him up in his arms. The boy recognized the man and hugged him fiercely, the two of them speaking rapidly in what Ruadhan knew to be Arabic. The man in rich robes carried the child away, and the spearmen encircled Ruadhan and Oliver once more.

"*Salaam aleikum,*" said Ruadhan cautiously.

"*Wa aleikum salaam,*" said a deep voice, and added, "*Yallah, askar.*" The spearmen stepped back and formed a line as a new man stepped forward. He was heavily bearded, and his eyes twinkled with humour. "Are you a Templar, by any chance?" the man asked.

"Why do you ask?" returned Ruadhan, and the man laughed.

"In my experience, it is only Templars, among all the Franks who live in this land, who bother to learn any Arabic at all," he replied. "Please, feel free to untie yourselves from your horses and get some clothes on. Your servant is unharmed, as are your horses. Fine steeds," the man added, "another sign that you're a Templar."

Ruadhan and Oliver turned their attention to the difficult work of untying the soaking knots around their waists. As they did so, the heavily bearded man said further things in Arabic to the spearmen, who trotted off across the sand. Two of them led the pair's horses back to them, along with a rather flustered Simon.

"I am sorry, milord. They came upon me suddenly, and I had no chance to fight," said the servant.

"I'm just glad that you have a whole skin, Simon," replied Oliver. "Do you have any idea who these fellows are?"

"I am Muqallad ibn Nasr ibn Sinan al-Kinani," said the heavily bearded man, "but you Franks will never manage that, so you may as well call me Nasr. And who might you be?"

"The sun shines on the hour of our meeting, Muqallad ibn Nasr ibn Sinan al-Kinani," said Ruadhan, inclining his head. "My name is Ruadhan Niall Noigiallach Ui Neill, of Ireland and the Poor Knights of Christ of the Temple of Jerusalem."

"Oliver Oakeshott, no fixed address," added Oliver.

The man called Nasr burst out laughing. "I have never met a Frank from Ireland, as far as I am aware," he said, "but I have heard that every man is as proud as a king on that far island. Well met, Ruadhan Niall Noigiallach Ui Neill. And Oliver Oakeshott. The sun does indeed shine on the hour of our meeting. So, what am I to do with the pair of you?"

"What do you mean?" asked Ruadhan. "We have done nothing to you or yours, and you have no claim on us."

Nasr, still smiling, said, "At any rate, there is no need for you to stand there shivering. I am being a poor host. Please accept my hospitality and follow me."

"May we ask what happened to the child and the two sailors?" pressed Oliver. "We saved their lives and would like to know."

"The boy has been happily reunited with his uncle, whom you just saw," said Nasr. "As for the sailors," he said, his expression darkening, "they are headed toward a different meeting."

"What do you mean?" asked Ruadhan.

"I mean that you have stepped into the middle of a story and need to hear at least a little more of it," replied Nasr. "If you will come with me, I will see how I can correct the situation."

---

Nasr's armed retinue worked quickly to erect a canopy tent on the grassland above the beach and then took trips back and forth from a line of pack horses to set out rugs and pillows as well as wine and fruit. *Whoever he may be,* Ruadhan reflected, *Nasr is not poor.* He and Oliver stripped off their soaking smallclothes and were given towels to wrap around their waists. Nasr invited them to recline on some pillows and enjoy some wine. Ruadhan sipped carefully; the wine was fruity and delicious and, in his exhausted condition, in danger of going straight to his head. Oliver drained his own cup and cheerfully asked for more.

The rescued child was sitting and chatting happily in Arabic with the man Nasr had called his uncle. Of the two men they had rescued, there was no sign.

Ruadhan and Oliver were offered grapes that were fresh and bursting with flavour. Oliver leaned back and stretched, his body languid despite his scarred musculature. "I could get used to living like this," he said happily, pouring himself more wine. "Are you planning on killing us, Nasr?"

The man's thick eyebrows rose. "Why would you think I plan to do that, Oliver Oakeshott?" he asked.

"Just the way things go, I suppose," replied Oliver, popping a grape into his mouth. "I've not experienced many random acts of kindness."

"And yet you have just created one," observed Nasr, gesturing towards the beach and the shipwrecked boat offshore. "Indeed, the pair of you risked your lives to achieve this act of kindness for the sake of people about whom you knew nothing."

"That was because of Ruadhan," said Oliver, waving his hand as if to signify that it was of no consequence.

Nasr looked at the Templar. "You have a remarkable power over your friend."

Ruadhan tried to avoid blushing, which only made it worse, so he said, "Tell us more about the story that we have stepped into today."

"Ah!" said Nasr, his eyes twinkling in a way that said he knew precisely what Ruadhan was doing. "It is not a particularly new or original story, but I suppose we can hardly hope for better in these times. The boy over there making himself sick on sweets is the child of a powerful lord. Not the heir, but important in his own right. A man decided to spit on his own oath of loyalty and kidnap the boy, planning on selling him to the family's enemies. This man was an idiot as well as a traitor and thought he would sail down the coast with his accomplices despite little experience of steering a ship. What happened next, you saw. On top of everything, the kidnappers were cowards and tried to save their own skins with no thought of the boy."

"We did not even know there was a child until the second time we went into the water," admitted Ruadhan. "The men we rescued said nothing. It was sheer luck we found him."

"Sheer luck that we found you, as well," added Nasr. "Those men would have murdered your servant and stolen your horses if we had not arrived when we did."

"Yet another argument against random acts of kindness," said Oliver, refilling his cup.

"And yet God moves in mysterious ways," replied Nasr. "He put us on that beach at exactly the right time for everyone involved."

"Except for the kidnappers," Oliver pointed out wryly.

"What kind of God would help such men?" asked Nasr, sipping his wine.

"What happens to them now?" asked Ruadhan.

"They face the lord they betrayed," Nasr replied. "I do not imagine it will be a pleasant reunion."

"Who is their lord? And your lord as well, I assume. I'm curious to know." Oliver plucked another grape.

Nasr smiled. "He is a man who rewards me for discretion. He will be pleased that this issue has been resolved without further incident. And he rewards you for your help in its resolution." Nasr signalled one of the spearmen, who came forward with a small chest about the size of a loaf of bread. He opened it to reveal that it was full of silver coins.

Oliver whistled. Ruadhan shook his head and said, "Your lord is too generous. Nasr, I have taken a vow of poverty. I would not be able to keep this for myself and would have to give it to my superiors."

"Just a moment now, don't be hasty," said Oliver, looking up at Ruadhan.

Nasr laughed. "Then I give it to your friend here," he said, pointing to Oliver. "I trust that he will be an excellent caretaker for the both of you and perhaps he will ensure that you live life a little more warmly than your cold Order ordinarily permits."

At a gesture from Nasr, the spearman handed the small chest to Oliver, who stood and accepted it with a small bow. "Thank you," said Oliver, "let us call this a payment towards a larger belief in random acts of kindness."

Nasr laughed and replied, "As you say. For my own part, I must believe in their power, or else my mission today would have ended in disaster. And now you must forgive us for our hasty hospitality, but we must be on our way to my master with the good news."

He stood up and gave several commands in Arabic, and his men hastened to carry out his orders. "I hope you will forgive me the over-familiarity, but I am leaving you with fresh underclothes," said Nasr. "You will not want dried salt water in certain places. Keep the towels, as well," he added, laughing.

With remarkable speed, Nasr's retinue broke down their camp and was on their way. Nasr leaned over his horse to say something to the boy, who then turned and waved back shyly.

Ruadhan and Oliver waved back, and soon, the group rode below a dip in the land and was gone from sight.

"Well, that's that, I suppose," said Oliver, sorting out his clothes. "I must say, Ruadhan, well done. Think what we would have missed if I hadn't listened to you. We'd be poorer, certainly." He gave the chest a shake and smiled at the sound of clinking coins.

Ruadhan pulled on his shirt. "Why did you?" he asked.

"Sorry, why did I what?"

"Listen to me," pressed Ruadhan. "You said to Nasr that you jumped in because of me. We risked our lives, Oliver. We could have died. You didn't have to follow me."

"Of course, I was going to follow you!" Oliver snorted, as if Ruadhan had said something ridiculous.

"Why?"

Oliver stepped into Ruadhan's space, his green eyes travelling from the Irishman's legs all the way up to his face. His lips parted slightly. "Because it was you," said Oliver simply.

"What?" Ruadhan felt lost, mesmerized by the intensity of Oliver's piercing eyes.

"You heard me," said Oliver, grinning as he stepped back and tied the small chest to the packhorse's saddlebags. "So where to? This has been a lovely spot for a picnic, but we should probably get moving."

"Uh...due north, by my reckoning," Ruadhan managed. "Follow the coast to Tripoli, stay long enough to rest and replenish our supplies, then we head for Shaizar and the Banu Munqidh."

"Sounds good," agreed Oliver, pulling himself up onto his horse. "Ready to go, Simon?"

"Yes, milord."

Ruadhan took the lead, not only because he had been to Tripoli before but also because he was trying to think without the distraction of looking at Oliver. The Englishman was a walking, talking, beautiful temptation. Ruadhan wanted to kiss him so badly that it hurt.

He knew that Oliver felt the same way. At times, the knight would tease him, as he had in the steam bath at the Templar commandery. Ruadhan had been certain that Oliver wouldn't make the first move, but neither would the man object to Ruadhan doing so. And just moments ago, he had been a heartbeat away from kissing Oliver, from seizing him in his arms and drowning himself in Oliver's sweet lips.

And then Oliver had smiled and moved away, not angry or disappointed, but teasing him playfully after telling Ruadhan that he would follow him anywhere.

*"Vivamus, atque amemus."* The words of Catullus, from centuries ago: "Let us live, and let us also love." Ruadhan had done his best to live, serving God and man as a Templar, but he had laid love aside long ago. In avoiding a fruitless marriage, he had done his best by his prospective bride, but what of himself?

Some members of his Order were keen to pursue an attraction between men – Gautier de Mesnil had made that very clear – but truth be told, there had never been anyone to whom Ruadhan had felt powerfully attracted.

Until Oliver. It had been something of a lonely existence, but Ruadhan had poured himself into his religious devotions and the development of his fighting skills. It had not really been enough, if Ruadhan was being honest with himself, but he had made it be enough.

Then, along came Oliver. He was everything that Ruadhan had ever wanted. Bright, clever, funny, daring, beautiful, and bursting with life. Someone who walked lightly through parts of living that Ruadhan struggled heavily with. Someone who was making it progressively clearer that he was Ruadhan's for the taking.

So, there it was. Clearly, the next move belonged to Ruadhan. What would he do?

*Poverty, chastity, and obedience. Those were the oaths I took.* Three simple things that involved a lifetime of discipline and denial. No one had forced him to take those oaths.

"But is that really true?" he muttered to himself out loud.

"What's that? You mumble like an old man," teased Oliver.

Ruadhan hastily pointed. "The Ladder of Tyre," he said, gesturing towards the sudden incline ahead.

"The what-of-what now?"

"This next section we need to cross," replied Ruadhan. They call it the Ladder of Tyre. We have to lead our horses carefully; it is steep and treacherous. Once we are on the other side of it, it will be a straight shot to Tripoli—three days, at most."

"Let's get to it, then," said Oliver. "The sun is already low; following this in the dark would be a beast."

"I had meant for us to be across it already," Ruadhan admitted, "but our seaside adventure delayed us."

"So, we're agreed. Next ship we see crash onto the shore, no stopping," said Oliver.

Ruadhan laughed.

The trio dismounted and carefully walked their horses up the steep and winding path. The terrain rose sharply, and the distance to the water crashing below grew great. Ruadhan focused on the pathway alone, but Oliver stopped every so often to peer over the ledge in the dwindling light.

"Great heaven, there are divers down there!" cried Oliver in astonishment. "What on earth are they doing, Ruadhan? They could be smashed to bits on those rocks! Look! Don't go jumping after them, mind," he added hastily.

Ruadhan looked down. "Those are snail divers," he said. "Come on, we must be off the Ladder before the light fails." Thankfully, they were near the top of the incline and would soon be journeying back down.

"You made that up," Oliver accused him. "There's no such thing as snail divers."

"Tyre is famous for its blue and purple cloth. The dyes come from sea snails," said Ruadhan, smiling. "The purple ones can be farmed, but the blue ones only grow wild and right in this area, for whatever reason. The tides make diving very dangerous, so there are only certain times that you can dive for them. Damned good swimmers, they have to be."

Oliver gaped at the divers, then back at Ruadhan. "This world never ceases to amaze me."

"It wasn't that long ago that you refused to leave Acre," observed Ruadhan.

"Ah, but that was before I met my guide to the wonders of the world," said Oliver, his eyes twinkling.

*I don't want to be without this man.*

The thought in Ruadhan's mind was as clear as spring water. None of the rest of his feelings – oaths, honour, the will of God – felt simple to the Irishman, but this one thing did. He knew this in his heart. The rest he would have to shape around this fact that was as hard as steel.

"What?" asked Oliver in amusement as he examined Ruadhan's expression.

"No great matter," said Ruadhan. "Some things become clearer on the road. Travel is a remarkable thing for the mind."

"Tell me about it," replied Oliver. "It took me hundreds of miles to figure out that my father is exactly the man I suspected him to be." He laughed. "Some people cast a long shadow."

"They do indeed," agreed Ruadhan. "Ah," he added as they reached the highest elevation point. "Good. Now, we start to descend. Keep your eyes on the trail; we should use the last remaining light to get down the Ladder."

"As you say. How are you doing back there, Simon?"

"Well enough, milord. The packhorse is a bit shy of this trail, but a little patience goes a long way," replied Oliver's servant.

"Good man."

They descended the far side of the Ladder of Tyre in relative silence, steering their horses along the trail as the sun set to the west. The Mediterranean Sea stretched as far as they could see on their lefthand side, and the shadows began falling on the fertile lands to their right. Many miles ahead of them, they could see the lights of the great city of Tripoli begin to twinkle in the twilight.

"You could travel for a very long time and not see anything as beautiful as this," said Oliver with a happy sigh.

*I know of something even more beautiful,* thought Ruadhan, but kept his peace.

The air was filled with small sounds: the crash of the waves far below them, the jingle of the horses' harnesses, the grate of hoofs against the rocky trail. As the trio turned through a switchback on the trail, Ruadhan lifted his hand to signal them to stop.

"We should light torches," he said. "The light will fail before we reach the bottom, and I have no desire to set up camp in darkness."

It took a few moments to kindle the torches, and they resumed their descent. With one part of his mind, Ruadhan guided his horse down the trail; the rest was occupied with the clarity of his earlier thoughts about Oliver. Ruadhan knew with certainty that he wanted to keep Oliver in his life. That was a beginning, surely?

*How would that even work? You are bound by oath to your Order; he has nothing to tie him to anything.*

That was where things became complicated.

As soon as Ruadhan moved away from his simple certainty, all of the difficulties entailed by his feelings came rushing out like a treacherous sea to twist him and pull him under, to make him despair at the impossibilities of his situation. Only when Ruadhan clung to what he knew to be true could he feel any sense of calm or peace .

Normally, this would be the point where Ruadhan would pray, and leave his uncertainties in the hands of God. But even that was treacherous; the Templar was not sure where God stood on the matter of love between men. It was a debate he had carried on within his own mind many times. Was this simply lust? Scripture had a great deal to say on the dangers of lusts of the flesh. Sexual desire within the bonds of marriage was an acceptable and proper thing, but if no sacrament of marriage existed between men, how could men ever be in the company of other men without sinning against God?

*Enough.*

Against these uncertainties, Ruadhan placed the certainty that he wanted Oliver in his life and did not want to lose him.

This much he knew. For the rest, he was trying to read the mind of God, and that was an attempt doomed to failure.

*I can still place all of this in God's hands. Lord,* he prayed, *I do not know if this love is pleasing in Your eyes, but I cannot believe that You are opposed to it. It is love; I know it in my heart. Your servant Paul tells us: And now abide faith, hope, love, these three; but the greatest of these is love.*

A wave of peace washed over Ruadhan, and he felt grounded in his faith and himself in a way he had not for a very long time. He lifted his torch and peered at the terrain.

"We're down the Ladder," he announced. "Let's look for a place to make camp."

## Chapter Thirteen
### OLIVER

The rest of the journey to Tripoli passed in relative simplicity. The trio were well supplied, first by Fabien and then later by Nasr, and the trip along the coast was far more pleasant than the desolate road from Acre to Jerusalem. It took them two more days to reach the great city, and each night, the lights of Tripoli appeared closer and closer. Finally, they could see the gates themselves in the morning light.

"Finally," said Oliver with relief. "I do prefer coastline to desert, but I prefer feather bed to rough ground even more."

"We can stop for at least a night in Tripoli," said Ruadhan in agreement. "I am sure the Templar commandery here will have decent lodgings."

"Commandery my arse," scoffed Oliver. "We have some pretty silver pennies thanks to Nasr, and I mean to spend some of them in this city."

Ruadhan laughed. "At the very least, I will pay my respects to the head of our chapter."

"Do they have a steam bath here?" asked Oliver, his face a study in innocence.

Ruadhan blushed. "No, that was a particular feature of the chapter house in Tyre."

"Pity."

Tripoli was dominated by its citadel, which stood frowning over the city, its high walls, and many towers ascending far above the shops and dwellings of the city proper.

Oliver whistled. "I would hate to be the soldier who had to attack that." It was one of the most impressive fortifications he had ever seen.

"It took Raymond of Saint-Gilles many long years of siege before the city of Tripoli was finally taken," said Ruadhan. "The citadel bears his name in his memory."

The trio joined the line of travellers seeking entrance to the city. Even the smaller city gates were of strong construction, and the sharp points of an iron portcullis hung above them as they passed into the city. The streets were loud and even busier than the markets of Acre and Tyre.

"I haven't seen anything like this since Constantinople," observed Oliver. "Not that Tripoli compares, really, but it's the closest since I came East."

"You should see Antioch," replied Ruadhan. "Over two hundred towers on the city walls alone."

"I apologize for ever thinking Outremer a backwater," laughed Oliver. "I had no idea. I thought Acre was the pinnacle of civilization beyond the sea." He eyed the sign of a nearby inn. "The Whistling Swallow. Looks likely enough."

"I would suggest that we hear the recommendations of my local knight commander before choosing any place in particular," said Ruadhan.

"Perhaps," said Oliver dubiously. "But if he says that the Whistling Swallow is a den of iniquity, just try and stop me."

They wove through the busy streets, Oliver keeping a sharp eye out for pickpockets and cutpurses. He would hate to lose Nasr's silver, at least without having a great deal more fun in the losing of it.

Finally, they reached the gates of the Commandery of Tripoli, and Ruadhan set his fist to the door set into the larger gate.

An eye slit slid back. "Who knocks?" demanded a voice within.

"Brother Ruadhan Ui Neill and his companions, reporting to Brother Evrard," replied the Irishman.

"Enter and be recognized," said the voice, and they heard the bolt slide as the door was opened.

"We cannot enter with our horses," said Ruadhan with a hint of impatience.

"Leave them outside," came the brusque reply.

Ruadhan looked back at Oliver, who raised his eyebrows and said nothing.

"This is poor courtesy," said Ruadhan, dismounting. A man in the livery of a Templar sergeant stepped through the door and eyed Ruadhan, Oliver, and Simon.

"I do but follow Brother Evrard's commands," replied the sergeant. "Your companions must wait here with your horses. You must follow me and see Brother Evrard."

Ruadhan sighed. "So be it."

Oliver had little patience for such rudeness and was tired, travel-worn, and hungry. "Meet us at the Whistling Swallow," he said irritably, "when you have finished with this charade."

Ruadhan nodded and went inside. The door shut, and Oliver could hear the sound of the heavy bolt as it slid home.

"The bigger the city, the ruder the people," Oliver said to

Simon. "Come on, let's backtrack to that inn. I need a proper drink."

---

It took Oliver and his servant a little while to rediscover the Whistling Swallow, and Oliver's irritation grew as they crisscrossed through the streets of Tripoli. Finally, they found themselves in front of the inn's stable yard, and Oliver practically jumped from his horse.

"Make sure the ostlers know what they're about and that the horses are tended to properly," he said, "then get yourself some food and drink. I'll see to some proper rooms."

"Yes, milord," replied Simon.

Oliver took a moment to stretch, then crossed the threshold of the inn. The experiences of the morning had left him in something approaching a foul temper. He had not appreciated the rudeness of the Templar sergeant, and now he was away from Ruadhan's side for the first time in days. He did not like the feeling. Oliver felt an ease in Ruadhan's company that he now missed. Simon was a superb traveling companion, of course, but Simon was not Ruadhan, not by a long road.

The inn's common room was decent enough and bore some signs of luxury and comfort. Fresh greenery hung from the rafters to give the air a pleasant scent, and the furniture was made of well-polished cedar. There were hangings on the walls that displayed the coats of arms of famous men who presumably had patronized the establishment. The emblems were unfamiliar to Oliver, but he assumed they belonged to local men of rank.

"And how may I help your lordship?" asked a slightly built

man who approached, touching his forelock. The man's face was open and honest, and Oliver immediately distrusted him as a matter of principle.

"I'm hungry, thirsty, and tired," Oliver announced with more arrogance than was customary for him. "Some food for me and my servant, some of your best wine, and two rooms for the night."

"Of course. May I ask how your lordship will be paying for these things?" said the man as he bowed slightly.

"I am a gentleman, good sir, and you may accept my word that your score will be paid," replied Oliver impatiently.

"It is the custom here in the city, milord, to make some deposit of coinage at the beginning of one's stay," said the innkeeper, bowing once more.

"Fine!" snapped Oliver. "My servant is in the stable yard; he will see that your needs are met." He sat down at a table with a thump. "Now, if it is not too much to ask, some food and wine, if you please."

He was quickly brought some fresh bread, roast chicken, and a cup of red wine, and he worked on these with vigour. As he began to ease his hunger, Oliver began to regret his earlier foul temper. He called the innkeeper over.

The man walked up to him, clearly nervous. "Has my servant settled accounts with you?" asked Oliver.

The man nodded cautiously. "Yes, milord."

"I am glad. I hope that you will forgive my earlier abruptness. My hunger got the better of my temper, I'm afraid. Your food is delicious and has entirely driven away my bad feelings," said Oliver.

Relief spread across the innkeeper's face. "I am glad to hear it, milord. If you still hunger, I will be happy to send you seconds."

"I don't suppose you have any fruit pie?" asked Oliver hopefully.

The man smiled. "Just cooling, milord."

"Heaven! What is your name, my man?"

"Ralph, milord."

"Ralph, you are a prince among men. Some more wine and a slice of pie when it is ready."

---

The pie was as good as Oliver hoped, and the wine was decent enough to go down easily. The more time passed, however, the more he began to wonder about his friend. Finally, he told Ralph to summon Simon, and Oliver regarded his servant moodily when he arrived.

"I hope you were able to eat and rest, Simon?"

"Yes, milord."

"Were you able to have some of that excellent pie?"

"No, milord."

"Ralph!" called Oliver. "A slice of pie for my servant here." The innkeeper nodded and hurried to obey.

Oliver waited in silence until Simon had had the opportunity to enjoy the pie. "Good, eh?" he asked.

"Delicious, milord," said Simon, wiping his mouth.

"I'm nervous, Simon."

"Milord?"

"Ruadhan should have been here by now. It makes me concerned that he is not," admitted Oliver.

"Would you like me to investigate, milord?"

"I think it might be best, Simon. Have you unpacked our things?"

"Not yet, milord."

"Then put them on the horses. Perhaps I'm being foolish, Simon, but I'm starting to wonder if something has gone amiss."

"As you wish, milord. I will prepare the horses and then ask after Brother Ruadhan." Oliver's servant got up and strode towards the stable yard.

Oliver himself tried to control his growing sense of unease. He called the innkeeper over.

"Milord?" asked the man.

"Ralph, have you lived in Tripoli for long?" asked Oliver.

"As long as I've lived in Outremer, milord. Twenty years if it's been a day," replied the innkeeper.

"What do you hear of Brother Evrard, the Templar Knight Commander?"

Ralph shrugged. "Brother Amaury was well beloved by many, milord. He died last year and was replaced by Brother Evrard—a hard man, I hear, but not a tyrant. Asks no more than his due, and he asks right to the copper. Gives what is his obligation to give, and not a copper more."

"Hmm. Thank you, Ralph," said Oliver.

"Milord." Ralph nodded his head and returned to his work.

Oliver began to heavily water his wine. If there was going to be trouble, he did not want to face it drunk.

Time continued to pass. Oliver's sense of unease grew.

It was well past noon when Simon returned to the common room, walking swiftly towards Oliver's table, his expression grim. The servant leaned over and murmured into his master's ear.

"We need to leave immediately, milord. A warrant for the

arrest of the companions of Brother Ruadhan Ui Neill has been issued."

Oliver stood up and strode toward the stable yard. "Where is Ruadhan?" he asked as they untied the horses.

"I don't know, milord," replied Simon. "As far as I could tell, still in the Templar commandery. There was no sign of him."

"Damn and blast," swore Oliver. "I don't want to leave him, but we can't help if we are all sharing a cell. Come on, let's head for the closest gate."

The pair left the stable yard and pushed through the busy streets. Oliver was sure that a cry would go up for their arrest at any moment, but instead, they steadily made their way through the crowd.

Suddenly the reins of his horse were seized, and Oliver was being led in a different direction. He looked down to see that a slender man with a short beard had his hands on the reins. The man looked up for a moment and said quite calmly, "You will never make it through the gates; a watch has been set on all of them. If you wish to avoid capture, go with me."

Oliver was about to protest when the man said, "If you wish to see your Templar friend alive again, you will do as I say."

Oliver glanced back quickly and saw another man leading Simon and his horse. Turning back to the figure with his hands on the reins of his horse, Oliver asked in a low voice, "Who has taken hold of my Templar friend?"

"His brothers," came the reply. "There are those among them who are faithless and corrupt."

Oliver and Simon were led down a side street and then another until they were well away from the crowded main streets. Oliver heard sudden shouting, and the men leading their horses began to jog.

"What is –"

"No talking now if you want to live," said the man, cutting Oliver off and gesturing for him to dismount. "Only following. Come with me. We will take care of your horses, but you two must come with me."

Oliver did as he was told. He reckoned that they had come this far, and he might as well see this path to its end. The second man who had been holding Simon's reins went off in a different direction with the horses, while the first man rushed Oliver and Simon into a rather unkempt dwelling.

The walls between houses appeared to have been knocked down as they travelled far further than Oliver thought possible for the single dwelling. Outside appearances were deceiving, for once they passed the front foyer of the house, the interiors were clean and richly appointed, with ornate mirrors and paintings on the walls and thick rugs under their feet.

Oliver had lost his bearings by the time they descended a set of stone stairs that led into a cool basement.

*I can't be in the same original house. How much farther am I from where I came in? What is this place? Where are we being taken?*

They passed from one basement chamber to another, which was furnished with a heavy table and a number of carved wooden chairs with plush cushions. Oliver was escorted to a chair, and Simon was directed to stand against a wall with a man on either side of him. Another man walked around the chamber, lighting the torches held in sconces on the walls.

Oliver sat down as a door on the opposite wall opened, and a man walked through. The man was remarkable in the sense that there was absolutely nothing remarkable about him. Oliver had never seen a man before who seemed to elude description or distinction in any way. The man sat down at the table opposite Oliver, folded his hands, and gave a quiet smile.

"Greetings, Sir Oliver Oakeshott," he said.

"Who are you?" demanded Oliver.

"I am known by many names," the man replied, "but you and your companions have been calling me Peter Thistle."

## Chapter Fourteen
### RUADHAN

"When will my companions be allowed inside the commandery?" asked Ruadhan as he followed the sergeant through the forecourt.

"You will have to take it up with Brother Evrard," the sergeant replied.

As they walked, Ruadhan's eyes were everywhere, trying to take in as much as possible. Unlike the commandery in Tyre, everything in Tripoli seemed tightly buttoned down; there were no animals in the forecourt, and the ground itself had been carefully swept. There were no sounds of conversation, and the sounds of their footsteps seemed unnaturally loud.

"Where are you taking me?" asked Ruadhan.

"To the Chapter Hall," said the sergeant. "Brother Evrard conducts all of his business there."

Ruadhan frowned but said nothing as he followed the sergeant through the corridors of the commandery until they reached a spacious chamber. The chamber had high vaulted ceilings with large windows that gave the room plentiful light. There were pews to either side, currently filled with members of the Order, all of them with their eyes on Ruadhan. At the far end of the room was a large oaken chair that was similar in appearance to a throne, and on either side of it a smaller chair. All three seats were occupied; the main one by a Templar with a neatly trimmed salt and pepper beard, a receding hairline, and eyes that glittered with malicious intelligence.

"You must be Brother Ruadhan," said the man in the oaken chair. He had an oddly high-pitched voice.

"I am," replied Ruadhan, putting a hand to his chest and bowing his head. "May I assume that you are Brother Evrard?"

"You may assume whatever you like, but if you do not address me by my title as Knight Commander of this Chapter, you will be put on bread and water rations for a week as a reminder of the importance of humility," said the man evenly.

Ruadhan hastily revised his understanding of what was going on. The man was clearly a martinet, and the Irishman would need to step very carefully to get out of his presence as quickly as possible.

"Forgive me, Knight Commander," said Ruadhan humbly, inclining his head once again. The silence that followed was clearly supposed to encourage him to speak further, but he was fully on guard now and offered nothing.

"So, what are you doing in my commandery, Brother Ruadhan?" asked Evrard eventually.

Ruadhan had no wish to discuss any business in the presence of the entire Chapter, but he was wary of making any protest. He had known Brother Amaury, a competent and pleasant Commander who was a confident leader of men, but this Brother Evrard seemed to be an entirely different case altogether. The atmosphere in the Chapter Hall was filled with an odd tension.

"Commander, I am here because I am in pursuit of a man named Peter Thistle," said Ruadhan. "I was given a mission to pursue and apprehend this man, and I have followed his trail to the city of Tripoli." All of this was entirely true, if not overly informative.

"Who sent you on this mission?" asked Evrard.

"Commander, I was given this mission by Brother Hugh Thomas, deputy of the Commandery of Acre, while we were escorting a caravan of pilgrims to Jerusalem."

Evrard frowned. "Highly irregular," he said. "Brother Hugh is not the Knight Commander of Acre, and he assigned you no companion."

"That is true, Commander," replied Ruadhan but offered no further explanation. For some reason, this Evrard seemed determined to find fault with him, and the Irishman was not interested in providing him with any further ammunition.

"Do you have any idea why Brother Hugh would have done such an irregular thing?" Evrard asked in a lazy drawl that bordered on insulting.

"I cannot speak for Brother Hugh, Commander," said Ruadhan, "but perhaps he felt the circumstances warranted such irregular orders."

"Don't play the fool with me, Brother Ruadhan," Evrard snapped. "It does not suit you and borders on insolence. I find the lash to be a strong corrective to an insolent tongue." His eyes glittered once more. "Do you require the lash, Brother Ruadhan?"

*What in God's name is going on here?*

"I do not, Commander. I apologize if I have offended. I am merely trying to speak with precision," said Ruadhan, casting his gaze downwards.

"Then employ your precision to answer my question, Brother."

"There had been a murder within the pilgrim caravan, Commander," said Ruadhan. "The man Peter Thistle was wanted for questioning. Brother Hugh assigned me to find him but did not want to send another Brother with me because we had already been attacked once, and he was concerned about future attacks. Therefore, he sent me with a secular knight to assist me in my pursuit."

"A secular knight?" Evrard frowned. "Most irregular."

Ruadhan waited him out.

"Despite the most unusual circumstances you have outlined, Brother Ruadhan, I suppose there is no reason to doubt the truth of what you have said." Evrard paused. "You have told us the truth, haven't you, Brother Ruadhan?"

The Irishman was careful to suppress his irritation at having his honesty called into question. "I have, Commander," he replied.

The smile that crawled along Evrard's mouth was cruel. "Condemned out of his own mouth, for the entire Chapter to hear," he said. "Send in Brother Gautier."

Ruadhan's blood went cold as Gautier de Mesnil walked into the room. Gautier locked eyes with Ruadhan and there was triumph in them as the Frenchman knelt humbly before the Knight Commander.

"He said exactly what you said he would say, Brother Gautier," said Evrard, continuing to smile. "A rogue and a coward, fleeing the Order and living in scandalous common with a secular knight. He shames us all."

"He knew exactly what I was going to say," said Ruadhan, barely curbing his fury, "because he was there to see it!

Commander, Brother Hugh Thomas will vouch for the truth of all that I have said!"

Evrard leaned forward. "But Brother Hugh is not here, is he? And I have no reason to doubt the word of a brave Templar knight who has shed his blood in the service of God and who has made the effort to shine the light of truth upon another man's lies."

The Knight Commander stood, and the Chapter stood with him. "Brother Ruadhan has been accused of grave crimes," Evrard announced. "Strip him of his habit and confine him to a cell as is laid out in our Rule. He is to be fed bread and water once a day and treated as a penitent. If he causes any difficulty, let the lash remind him that he is subject to our discipline. He is to remain confined until Brother Hugh Thomas may be brought forth to speak to his guilt or innocence. Go to the secular powers and inform them that we wish an arrest warrant to be issued for Brother Ruadhan's companion and his servant. We will seek jurisdiction over them insofar as their conduct affects the good name of the Order. This Chapter is concluded."

Ruadhan stood open-mouthed, unable to process the speed at which the disaster had occurred. Firm hands stripped him of his Templar habit, leaving him in a light cotton shift. His weapons were carried away, and he was marched down a corridor, then down a twisting set of stone steps until he faced a small cell containing some bedding and a chamber pot and nothing else.

"In," said one of the Templar knights escorting him. Ruadhan had to duck to enter; the cell was less than the height of a man.

"May you spend your time in prayer and come swiftly to an acknowledgement of your sins," intoned the same man.

"Without true penitence, there can be no forgiveness." He closed the small wooden door and left Ruadhan in darkness.

---

The air felt thick and hard to breathe, and Ruadhan had to concentrate to slow his breathing down and avoid the panic that threatened to rise up and choke him.

*How had this happened?*

Clearly, the Knight Commander was a petty tyrant who lorded it over the Brothers who were unfortunate enough to serve under him. That, however, had not been enough to see him into this lightless cell. That had been the work of Gautier de Mesnil.

*Why had Gautier done it?* All other things being equal, the matter would be cleared up when Hugh Thomas was reached and could attest to the truth of what Ruadhan had said. At that point, Gautier himself would be in a great deal of trouble and, under the Rule, could be liable to the charge of false accusation and possible expulsion from the Order.

Ruadhan sat down on the bedding, stretching his legs out. Thankfully, the cell had enough width that he was able to extend them fully, even if he could not stand up straight. *He must have been desperate*, Ruadhan realized. Gautier had needed to slow Ruadhan and Oliver down, and that had justified the risk of making an accusation that bought the Frenchman a little time, although what Gautier needed the time for, Ruadhan had no idea. It was a move of desperation, meaning they must have been very close to discovering something.

*But what?*

A chill passed through Ruadhan as he realized that the only

way for Gautier to emerge from this situation unscathed was for Hugh Thomas to die. It would also be far more convenient for the devious Frenchman if Ruadhan never emerged from this cell.

This was meant to be a death trap.

---

Ruadhan had no way of telling how much time was passing, so it could have been minutes or hours later when his grim thoughts were interrupted by a tap of the wooden door that stood between him and freedom. A slot near the bottom of the door slid back.

"Well, Brother," said Gautier, "you seem to have gotten yourself into a fine mess."

"There is nothing I wish to say to you," replied Ruadhan through gritted teeth. "Your lies will be discovered soon enough."

"You're a clever enough man, Brother Ruadhan," said Gautier. "You will already have realized that I will never let Brother Hugh come here to testify on your behalf, let alone let you leave this cell. This rotten little hole is where you will die."

"Mere words," sneered Ruadhan, but despair gripped his heart. In truth, he was helpless. His fate was out of his hands.

"Not just words, Brother Ruadhan," said Gautier lightly. "You know my intentions. How could you possibly trust the bread or water passed through this door, knowing I am on the other side of it? No, you have perhaps two, maybe three days before your thirst drives you to drink poison. As a kindness, I have ensured you will not even taste it. Or maybe there is no poison, and the water is perfectly safe?" The Frenchman laughed softly.

"Gautier?"

"Yes, Brother?"

"In the name of Heaven, why are you doing this?" Ruadhan demanded.

"You must take me for a fool," snapped Gautier, slamming the slot shut. Ruadhan heard the muffled sound of his footsteps walking away, and then there was silence.

---

The cell posed far more danger to Ruadhan's mind than his body. It was cold, damp, and bug-ridden, but these challenges were nothing new to the Irishman. He had endured this much and worse while on campaign. The constricted size of the cell could become a problem, he knew, but he was being careful to stretch his limbs so that his muscles did not cramp or spasm. He had precious little else to do, after all.

The weight that pressed upon Ruadhan was a creation of his senses and his mind. He was in near total darkness and close to total silence. The ability to tell the passage of time disappeared quickly. He could track it if he counted, but it slipped away unless he was actively counting. Ruadhan knew that life and death struggles could take place less than a city block away, but they belonged to a different world. His world was now this cell.

Some time later, he once more heard the sound of muffled footsteps, then the sound of the slot sliding open and the scrape of something on the floor.

"I must speak to Brother Evrard," he tried to say, but it came out as a rasping croak.

He was ignored, and the slot slammed shut. The footsteps walked away, and silence returned. Ruadhan felt panic rise in his chest once more. It might have been different if there had been anything to fix upon – a torch to light the darkness, another person to talk to, the ability to see or hear anything other than his wretched self. But there was nothing except Ruadhan, the bread he dared not eat, and the water he dared not drink.

## Chapter Fifteen
### OLIVER

Oliver sat and stared in stupefaction at the man who claimed to be the object of their mission. He was entirely unremarkable; a small, neatly trimmed beard covered the lower half of a face whose features could have come from any number of Mediterranean peoples from Marseilles to Cairo. Even his eyes seemed blandly pleasant and neutral as they regarded Oliver with just a hint of amusement.

"I take it you are not a cooper from Acre," said Oliver.

The man shook his head. "I am not," he admitted. "Would it shock you to know that my name is not even Peter Thistle? Although it is close to what my brothers call me; to them, I am known as *Shawka* – Thorn, as you would say."

"Your brothers?" asked Oliver.

The man who called himself Thorn raised an eyebrow. "Surely you have figured that out by now, Sir Oliver."

"If I had to guess, I would say that you and your brothers are Assassins," said Oliver, "but I must admit that I'm at the point where I feel certain about very little."

Shawka flashed a white-toothed smile. "Some say that is the beginning of true wisdom."

"I am certain that I want my friend back," returned Oliver. "That much I do know."

"Be at peace, Sir Oliver. My brothers have set the wheels in motion for his freedom."

"I'm going to need a little more than that, Master Shawka, or I will thank you for your help and be on my way to rescue my friend myself," said Oliver.

Shawka nodded. "By all accounts, you are a brave warrior, Sir Oliver, and I have no doubt that many Templar knights would fall before your blade. But do you really think you can fight through all the Templars of Tripoli to find your friend?"

Oliver gave a small smile. "I think that I would kill more than most people could imagine."

"And your friend, who right now lies in a cell beneath the commandery?" asked Shawka gently. "Would he survive to be rescued?"

"Probably not," Oliver admitted, folding his arms.

"Then may I suggest that you wait while my brothers and I bring our plans to bear upon your friend's situation?"

"I would feel a great deal better about doing so," said Oliver, "if I understood why you and your brothers would want to help us."

"And so we come to the heart of things," said Shawka, smiling. "While my brothers prepare, let us enjoy something to eat and some *qahwa* to drink, and I can help you understand what you and your friend have walked into."

"*Qahwa?*" asked Oliver.

"It is a beverage that is made –" began Shawka, but Oliver raised a hand to stop him.

"I know what it is," said Oliver, "and it's the first sensible suggestion anyone has made in quite a while."

---

A short time later, the table in the cellar chamber was adorned with a number of small plates containing a variety of fruits and sticky sweets, as well as an ornate pot filled with hot, fresh *qahwa*. Oliver took a few sips of the piping hot liquid from a delicate cup and regarded Shawka with a considerably more friendly demeanour.

"Tell your story, Master Thorn," he said with an expansive gesture.

Shawka sipped his own drink. "Where to begin," he said. He turned to one of his companions and said something in Arabic; the man nodded and left the room. "It is easier if I begin by showing you," said Shawka by way of explanation. The man returned and laid what had to be a weapon on the table between the Assassin and the English knight. Oliver looked at it in fascination.

It appeared to be a very small yet powerful bow, laid on its side and attached to a thick stock of wood. A metal groove ran down the stock, and there looked to be some sort of trigger mechanism on the bottom side.

"It fires these," said Shawka, taking a short, thick arrow from the man and handing it to Oliver. It was heavy in Oliver's hands, and it had stiff fletching and a razor-sharp head. The Englishman eyed the powerful arms of the bow section dubiously. "No man could pull and hold that," he said.

"They don't have to," said Shawka confidently. He held up what looked like an iron poker with a claw at its head. "You pull back with this until the string is over the trigger mechanism. The stock holds the tension until you pull the trigger, firing the arrow."

"And a man with a regular bow could fire any number of arrows while you're pulling the strong back, aiming, pulling the trigger," said Oliver skeptically.

"True," Shawka agreed. "But this special bow can punch through armour at two hundred yards. Armour of proof at one hundred."

Oliver's jaw dropped as he imagined the effect of a single volley of one hundred or two hundred of these bows firing at a mass of charging knights on horseback.

*A massacre.*

"Where does...where does this thing come from?" he managed.

"From the East," Shawka replied. "Very far. They've been using it for a long time. They call it a *nu*. We call it *aqqar*. In your tongue, I believe it is called a *crossbow*."

Oliver shook his head. "This could change the face of battle forever," he said.

"Certainly, the Venetians hope so," replied Shawka. "As do the Genoese and the Pisans."

"What?" exclaimed Oliver in disbelief.

"Let me try and help you to imagine it," said the Assassin, putting his hands on the table. "The Italian cities are filled with merchants and sailors. Powerful enough in their own way, but their strength has never been in their land armies. They cannot compare to the armoured knights of France, of the Empire, or even your own England. How long does it take to train a knight, Sir Oliver?"

"I was taught from the time I could ride," answered Oliver, "when I was very small."

"A man can be trained to be deadly with a crossbow within a month," said Shawka.

Once more, Oliver shook his head. "God in Heaven," he muttered. "Years of training, a fortune in horses, armour, and weapons, ended in an instant by a peasant with shit behind his ears."

"Precisely," said Shawka. "For us, it matters little; our strength has never been in fixed battle and never will be. But when the Italians heard of, then saw the crossbow, they were not fools. They recognized its value. They want as many of these things as we can sell to them."

"So that's what all of this has been about? Money?" asked Oliver.

"When is it ever about anything else?" asked Shawka rhetorically. "We have something that others want. We can make a great profit from this, and we are always in need of money, thanks to those bastard Templars who force us to pay them a fortune in tribute every year."

"So, the Templars are trying to stop you from selling crossbows to the Venetians?" Oliver's brow furrowed.

"Hah!" shot back Shawka. "They have no problem with us doing this as long as the Temple gets its cut. Those bastards want us to sell crossbows to *them* for pennies, and *they* will sell the crossbows to the Venetians at a much higher price. Always, always, the Temple keeps us beneath their heel by starving us of money."

"All right," said Oliver, "I can understand this. I can see how this has happened. But what does it have to do with me? Why were you a part of the caravan to Jerusalem, pretending to be a pilgrim? Hard to imagine you as a cooper, by the way."

Shawka grinned. "As it happens, I was a cooper's apprentice for a time. I was with the caravan to meet Arnaldo, the Venetian silversmith. He was an emissary from his city, sent to negotiate with us for the sale of crossbows. He was to give me a token – a silver apple pendant – as a sign that he was who he said he was." The Assassin sighed. "He was not as careful as he should have been. I spotted the pendant hanging from his neck, as did some of his fellow pilgrims. So did the bastard Templar who murdered him before I could make contact."

"A Templar murdered Arnaldo?" exclaimed Oliver.

"There is a group of Templars who have made it their duty to always watch us and ensure that we have very little room to breathe. It is their policy to make their Order rich by squeezing us dry. The man who murdered Arnaldo is well known to us. A very dangerous Templar, who has been a blade in our side ever since he set foot in this land," said Shawka. "A knight named Gautier de Mesnil."

"That bastard," breathed Oliver.

"He murdered Arnaldo and made sure the boy and his mother, who had also seen the pendant, died. He took the pendant from Arnaldo's body, and I suspect he still has it. I think his original plan was to pretend to be my contact or to pass it on to another Templar spy to do the same."

"So why did you tell Brother Hugh about the pendant when he questioned you?" asked Oliver.

Shawka shrugged. "I hoped that they would find it amongst Gautier's possessions and know that he was involved. For myself, I knew that I had to escape. After I told Brother Hugh that I had seen the pendant, I knew Gautier would try and murder me in the night. I was just preparing to flee when you came walking up to my tent."

"You mean you were the one who knocked me out?" Oliver demanded.

The Assassin spread his hands in a conciliatory gesture. "I am sorry and hope that you can forgive me, Sir Oliver. Many things were uncertain at that time, and I could not be sure that you were not meant to be my murderer. For whatever it may be worth, I am very glad that I did not kill you."

"That brings us to here and now," said Oliver, setting aside for the moment that Shawka had struck him down all those days ago. "Why did you rescue my servant and me? Why are you putting things in motion to help my friend Ruadhan?"

"At first, my only thought was getting away from you," admitted Shawka. "You nearly had me in Tyre, you know! I felt you nipping at my heels." He grinned. "Fortunately, hashish tends to change the nature of people's perceptions for just long enough to be very helpful."

"So, you were the one who tried to have my body rearranged by those ruffians in the marketplace," Oliver observed.

Shawka repeated his earlier conciliatory gesture. "I did not know who you were nor why exactly you were pursuing me. You could have just as easily been minions of Brother Gautier."

Oliver nodded. "True."

"But then," Shawka continued, "you rescued a child, and that changed everything."

"You mean the business with the ship and that Nasr fellow?" Oliver's eyebrows rose. "That was all Ruadhan; he was practically in the water before I knew what was happening. Who in God's name *was* that child? Nasr played his cards very closely about what exactly had happened, but it looked like we had saved two men from drowning only for them to find death on shore."

"No less than those traitors deserved," said Shawka. "I cannot go into detail without betraying the confidences of others, but let me simply say that the boy you saved is very important to the future of the community I serve. With your actions, Sir Oliver, you and Brother Ruadhan placed my community into your debt."

"And by your community, you mean..." began Oliver.

"Those whom you call Assassins," finished Shawka. "We call ourselves Nizaris, the Banu Munqidh call us Batinis, but for you Franks the term 'Assassins' will do. In the end, we all carry many names."

"I'm just Oliver," the knight replied.

Shawka laughed. "If that were true, you would not have travelled such a long way to escape the name Oakeshott," he observed.

There was a brief silence, and then Oliver leaned back. "I thought this before, and now you confirm it: you are frighteningly well-informed."

"When everyone else in the world hates you and wants you dead, you have to be well informed if you want to survive," returned Shawka. "But that is not what presses us right now. What is before us is the fact that the authorities are pursuing two men to whom my community is indebted, and that one of them has been shoved in a cell at the bottom of Tripoli's Templar commandery." Shawka looked past Oliver for a moment. "Two men and their loyal servant, I should say."

"Simon, you must be famished," said Oliver, turning around. "You need food and drink."

"I would prefer to listen and learn if it pleases you, milord," said Simon.

Turning back to face Shawka, Oliver said, "He's really less of a servant and more of a travelling spirit of mild disapproval."

"If you say so," laughed the Assassin.

"So please, tell me what you know of Ruadhan," pressed Oliver. "Have they hurt him? What is his condition? And how do you know?"

"They have not harmed him, yet. He refuses food and water because he fears poison. The cell is unpleasant and designed to make the occupant despair, but Brother Ruadhan is holding up. There is cause for concern, however; Brother Gautier is there and has the Knight Commander's ear."

"Gautier! I'll wring his neck with my bare hands," swore Oliver. "I should have known that snake would be in the thick of it. Thank you for answering my questions, Shawka, but you have not answered all of them. How do you know all this?"

"Do you know what a *fida'i* is, Sir Oliver?" asked Shawka.

"No idea."

"There are members of our faith who, to serve God and our leaders, go out into the world and live as those around them do. They work, they pray, they build lives as Sunni Muslims, Shi'a Muslims, and even Christians. But they are faithful, Sir Oliver; faithful to their true beliefs, and they remain ready to serve the Nizaris at a moment's notice, even to the point of sacrificing their lives if need be." Shawka spread his hands. "The *fida'i* are everywhere."

"I have heard tell of this. Do you have men even in the Templar commandery?" Oliver asked, staggered at the implications of Shawka's words.

"Even there."

"God in Heaven," Oliver breathed.

"This is why, although we are feared and hated, we are not destroyed," said Shawka. "People step carefully and think twice when their very own servants might have a knife or poison."

Oliver turned to look at Simon. "You're not an Assassin, are you?"

"No, milord."

"That's what he would say if he was an Assassin, wouldn't he?" Oliver asked Shawka, who chuckled and said, "Alas, your Simon is not one of our own."

"Which is what you'd say even if he was," observed Oliver. "Mother Mary! What a way to live. No wonder everyone is terrified of you. Except the Templars, apparently. And the Hospitallers."

"It is true," admitted Shawka. "They pledge their lives to their cause, and it does not matter to them whether they die in battle or by the murderer's blade, as long as they die in service to their God. There is no threat that we can make against such men."

"So how do we rescue my friend?" asked Oliver. "He's in the middle of these people, and at least one of them wants him dead."

"It is a bad situation," admitted Shawka. "My community reaches everywhere, but our reach is most limited within Templar walls. I know for certain that we can get him out of his cell, but past that, it becomes far more difficult."

"Get him out of his cell," said Oliver, "and I can get him the rest of the way."

"You do not lack for confidence," said Shawka, smiling. "But I think we can do better than that."

# Chapter Sixteen
## RUADHAN

Sleep was becoming difficult, if not impossible. His back was sore and bloody from where they had lashed him.

At first, Ruadhan had refused food and water, fearing poison. When this news reached Brother Evrard's ears, Ruadhan was dragged from his cell and ordered to eat.

"You belong to the Order," Evrard had said. "You do not have the right to damage the property of the Temple."

When Ruadhan still refused, Evrard had ordered him strung up in the Chapter Hall and wielded the whip himself. In the end, Ruadhan had eaten on his knees in front of the Knight Commander and then been shoved back into his cell. The entire affair had been humiliating, but Ruadhan had reckoned that if any food and water was going to be safe, it would be that which came straight from the hands of the Commander; Gautier would not dare poison it. A bloody back was worth getting sustenance that he could trust.

Ruadhan tried not to think about his next confrontation with the Commander, if he once again refused to eat and drink what was brought to his cell. Brother Evrard was a sadist, that much was clear, and the man would secretly delight in Ruadhan's defiance as an opportunity to punish him further.

It was hard not to fall into despair, locked away in his cramped little cell below the surface of the world. He had no idea how long he had been here. *Was it a day? Two days? More?* Ruadhan had blinked at the brightness of the light when he had been dragged in front of Brother Evrard. It had been morning when he had first walked into the Commandery, and he was fairly sure that many further hours had passed before his whipping.

*Did that make this the second day? Or longer?*

Ruadhan's thoughts fled when he heard the sound of footsteps in the hallway outside his cell. If this was food, did he dare refuse it? What if it was Gautier? Would the Frenchman murder him here, where no one else would see or know of it?

*I wish I could see Oliver one more time, just to say goodbye.*

The slot at the bottom of the door slid back. "I am going to unlock the door," said a voice. "Do not attack me. I am here to help. I have with me your armour and weapons. You must put them on quickly and follow me."

Ruadhan was filled with confusion, and he sat hunched in the cell as he heard the sound of the door being unlocked. Then the door swung open, and the little space was filled with torchlight. Ruadhan squinted up at the figure behind the torch and asked in a gravelly voice, "Who are you?"

"A friend," came the reply. "Please hurry! We do not have much time."

*Even if this is a trick, the alternative is to sit here and rot.* "I will need your help," he croaked. "I may not be able to raise my arms above my head."

The stranger with the torch gave a hiss and a quiet curse as

Ruadhan emerged from the cell and turned to show the state of his back. The Irishman gasped in pain as the man worked his arms up, breaking the scabs along his shoulders and letting fresh blood flow.

Finally, Ruadhan was clad once more in his long coat of mail, although the skin along his upper body felt as though it was on fire. The stranger helped him with his sword belt, and as Ruadhan grasped the hilt of his sword, he felt a sudden rush of murderous rage against the men who had rendered him helpless.

The wave of energy that came with his anger gave Ruadhan strength, and he nodded at the man with the torch, who looked anxiously at him. "Follow me," said the stranger, who was clad in the habit of a Templar sergeant.

"Who are you?" Ruadhan asked, but the man shook his head impatiently and said, "No time. I am a friend. Be as quiet as you can."

Ruadhan followed his rescuer through the corridor. It was very short, no more than twenty paces, despite the huge distance it had assumed in his mind. At the end of the corridor was another door, which the man opened, and then a set of stairs leading upward towards freedom.

Already, the air felt fresher upon Ruadhan's face as they ascended the stairs and moved as quietly as they could through the Chapter Hall. Almost involuntarily, Ruadhan looked down to see if any spatter of blood remained from his whipping, but the stones had been washed clean.

The pair emerged into the courtyard, and Ruadhan looked up to see the stars glittering brightly on a night with a luminous moon. His rescuer paused and leaned over to whisper something in Ruadhan's ear.

Instead, Ruadhan heard Brother Evrard say, "Now, please," and the courtyard was alight as hoods were pulled from multiple lamps. Between the pair and the gate stood a gathering of Templar knights and sergeants, all armed. At their head stood Brother Evrard. The Knight Commander was smiling as he regarded Ruadhan.

"Brother, how badly you have strayed," he said in his high voice. "And you have now corrupted a good sergeant as well. No matter. We will see you both purified." Evrard lifted his hand. "Take them both alive."

Before the Knight Commander could lower his hand, the air was filled with the sound of low thrumming followed by zipping noises, like bats flying close by, and the heads of several Templar knights exploded. Ruadhan stared as several men fell like marionettes with cut strings—squat, ugly arrows protruding from their shattered skulls.

The Irish Templar watched as a man leapt from the wall down to a set of stairs and from the stairs to the ground of the forecourt. Ruadhan laughed with joy as he recognized Oliver Oakeshott, who drew his sword and struck a Templar knight in the face with the pommel of his sword. The man went down with a cry, holding both hands to his eye.

"Who wants to face me?" cried Oliver, his face red with anger in the torchlight. "You filthy cowards, come on!" The knight's fury emanated from him like a physical force, and the assembled Templars and sergeants stepped back.

"I'm not afraid of you." Brother Evrard's high voice cut through the night. The Knight Commander stepped forward. "You perverted demon. Through my hand, God will cut you down."

"No," said Ruadhan, who drew his sword as those gathered

in the forecourt turned to face him. "Brother Evrard, you face me. Let's see how you fare when we fight man to man."

"Anyone who thinks to interfere will face an arrow to the face," called Oliver. "My archers stand ready."

"Brother Ruadhan," said Brother Evrard mockingly. "A sinner, a liar, and a vessel for lust." He drew his sword. "I should have whipped you harder to scourge the Devil from your overstained soul. I will pray for you even as your spirit writhes in Hell."

"Any God that would listen to your prayers is not worthy of the name," returned Ruadhan through gritted teeth. He gripped his sword in both hands, keeping his weight on the balls of his feet as he stepped forward. Brother Evrard smiled at him, and anger threatened to choke off Ruadhan's breath, but he deepened his breathing and found calm once more.

Even as he did so, Brother Evrard lashed out with a thrust at Ruadhan's face that was shockingly quick, faster than he would have thought the man was capable of. Ruadhan barely managed to move his head out of the way in time, and when the Knight Commander shifted his thrust into a sideways slash, he struck Ruadhan in the side of the head heavily enough that the Irishman briefly saw spots discoloring his vision. The only thing that saved Ruadhan's life was his chainmail hood.

Brother Evrard did not stop there, spinning his body to turn his backstroke into a spinning backhand slash at Ruadhan's abdomen. The Knight Commander continued to smile, his face a rictus of vicious mockery as his blade whipped around. Ruadhan dropped his sword into a weak parry that managed to keep the attack from sinking into his belly, even as Brother Evrard stamped his foot and reversed his spin, turning his blade around as if it weighed no more than a length of cord and making a deadly downward stroke aimed at Ruadhan's head.

The speed of the man's attacks gave Ruadhan no time to think; all he could do was retreat and defend himself with increasing desperation. Brother Evrard's smile grew wider. Ruadhan wasn't sure how much space remained between his retreating body and the wall, but he knew that his room to maneuver was shrinking rapidly.

Suddenly, a thought passed through Ruadhan's mind, as clear as the tolling of a church bell: *He is a bully. He lives on your fear. As long as you are afraid of him striking you, it is only a matter of time before he lands a killing stroke.*

Realizing this, the Irishman suddenly smiled. He had been dealing with bullies all his life, and this vicious sadist did not deserve his respect or his fear. Brother Evrard looked at his expression with uncertainty and misstepped slightly, even as Ruadhan turned defence into attack. Their swords rang as their blades collided again and again.

Ruadhan deliberately allowed his attacks to fall into a pattern, hoping Brother Evrard would take the bait. The Irishman watched his opponent's eyes flicker as the man prepared to make a sudden move, but before the Knight Commander could do so, Ruadhan shifted to a single-hand grip and punched Brother Evrard in the face with his free hand. He felt the man's nose break under his mailed fist and the crack of shattering teeth.

Ruadhan's opponent staggered back.

In an instant, Ruadhan knew the man's next move: to drop his sword and yield. Brother Evrard was a serpent who wanted to slither back under his stone, to emerge and show his fangs another day.

*You're out of time.*

Ruadhan gripped his sword in two hands once more and thrust the blade directly into Brother Evrard's chest, using all of his strength to force the blade through broken links of mail, past the leather beneath, and to break bone as he pushed the steel into the Knight Commander's heart.

Brother Evrard's eyes went wide, and he dropped his sword as his hands clenched and unclenched convulsively. Then he went to his knees, retched up blood, and fell.

Ruadhan put his foot to the dead man's chest and planted it there for leverage as he pulled his blade from the man's body. He turned to face the gathered knights and sergeants, his blade dripping with the heart's blood of their Knight Commander, as they regarded him in stunned silence.

"Right," said Ruadhan, "who's next?"

Oliver's footsteps were loud in the silence as he walked forward to stand beside his friend, shoulder to shoulder, and lifted his blade in readiness.

"Whoever wishes to die, step forward," challenged the Englishman.

The air rang with the clanging sounds of dropped blades, and the surviving Templars fell to their knees.

Ruadhan looked at Oliver. The killing fury faded from the knight's eyes, and he turned to look at Ruadhan, his expression lightening as ferocity was replaced by mirth.

"Know any good sword merchants?" asked Oliver. "There's a fortune on the ground here."

They quickly marched the disarmed Templars into the refectory, a grim and joyless chamber of stone with high, narrow windows and only two doors, which they could lock with keys Ruadhan confiscated from the commandery's Seneschal. "We'll be gone by morning," Ruadhan informed the officer, "so do not think to try and make your escape before then. We see any of you outside the refectory, and we'll kill you."

"You will be expelled from our Order," spat the Seneschal. "Your lives will be forfeit for what you have done."

Ruadhan laughed bitterly. "Do you think I would remain a part of any Order that would do to me what your Knight Commander did?"

"We but obeyed our lawful commanding officer, just as the Rule demands," protested the Seneschal.

"Which makes you as contemptible as him," replied Ruadhan. "If I see you again, I'll kill you." He shut the door in the Seneschal's face and turned the key.

Ruadhan and Oliver returned to the forecourt to deal with the last remaining Templar. Gautier de Mesnil was still on his knees, sobbing quietly as he clutched at his face. Blood ran from where his hand covered his right eye socket.

"We have business with this man," said Shawka, emerging from the shadows of the courtyard. He was flanked by several men with cloth-covered faces, each carrying a crossbow.

"Ruadhan," said Oliver, "may I introduce to you Master Shawka of the Assassins, also known as –"

"Peter Thistle," finished Ruadhan. "I recognize you from our first encounter. Well met, Master Shawka. I take it we have you to thank for my rescue."

Shawka gave a small bow. "I was happy to assist, Brother Ruadhan."

"Not Brother. Not anymore. My time with the Templars is done," said Ruadhan.

"As you say," replied Shawka. "I do not think you will be diminished by the end of your association."

"I'm coming to realize that very fact, Master Shawka," observed Ruadhan. "What do you want with this wretch?" he asked, gesturing to the kneeling Gautier.

Shawka walked up to the stricken Templar and crouched before him. "Brother Gautier," he said softly. "Brother!" He shook Gautier's shoulder. "You have something that was meant for me. A token. It is not yours to keep, and you must return it now."

Gautier kept his face pointed downwards as he put a shaking hand beneath his surcoat, pulled out a chain with a silver apple pendant, and lifted it towards the Assassin. Shawka held the pendant pulled sharply, snapping the chain and making the Templar flinch. He walked back towards Ruadhan and Oliver and showed them the pendant.

It was a beautiful piece of craftsmanship; a miniature replica of an apple made entirely of silver. Shawka dropped it into Ruadhan's hand, and he felt the weight of it as he raised it to examine it more closely.

"There is writing on it," said Ruadhan, peering at an inscription in what he guessed was Arabic.

"It is the guiding principle of my community," replied Shawka. "It says: 'Nothing is true. All is permitted.'"

Oliver's eyes widened. "What a way to look at the world," he said.

Shawka grinned. "You should try it for yourself sometime. We walk a path to freedom, which is why we are hated by everyone. Keep the pendant, Sir Ruadhan, as a memento of this experience and a sign of goodwill should you meet any of my people again. That is if you can even recognize them for who they are. As for this fellow," he said, pointing to Gautier, "we shall take him with us. Brother Gautier seems to know more than is good for him, and we will invite him to share that knowledge with us."

Shawka said something in Arabic to his companions, too quick for Ruadhan to try to follow. One of the masked men stepped forward. "Follow this man, gentle sirs," said Shawka. "He will take you beyond the walls where your servant waits with your horses and supplies. It would not be a good idea for you to remain in the city or anywhere near it."

"Master Shawka," said Ruadhan, shaking his head, "thank you for everything. We are indebted to you."

"Nonsense!" cried the Assassin, smiling. "I do but repay a debt incurred by a random act of kindness. A very powerful thing, but now our slate is clean. Perhaps we shall see each other again." Shawka gave another small bow and turned away to deal with his men and the unfortunate Gautier de Mesnil.

---

Their silent guide took them through side streets and back alleys until they reached a small postern gate set next to a culvert that brought fresh water into the city. They did not speak and moved carefully, listening for any sounds of discovery. Their guide unlocked the gate and led them down a set of stairs, then through a tunnel that passed under the thick stone of the city wall. They emerged through another small door on the other side and found themselves outside the city.

"Honestly, I don't know why anyone bothers to use a front

gate anymore," whispered Oliver, and Ruadhan had to put his sleeve to his mouth to stop himself from laughing. Their guide stared them both into silence, and the three of them loped through the night at a gentle jog until, about half a mile from the city walls, they saw a group of horses and a familiar figure.

"Simon," said Ruadhan with deep affection, "I thought I might not see you again."

"Well met, milord," replied Simon gravely. "I am glad to see you whole."

"We are all whole, which is more than I thought we could hope to say," said Oliver. "Thank you, mysterious guide, for bringing us here." Apparently immune to irony in a foreign tongue, their masked companion nodded and set off at a jog back into the night towards the city.

"So," said Oliver, "here we are. All alive and free, which is good, but what in the name of Heaven do we do now? The Templars will want to kill us, doubtless; the Count of Tripoli has issued a warrant for our interest. It is hard to imagine that we will find many welcomes."

"Nothing is true. All is permitted," said Ruadhan thoughtfully.

"Very interesting, on a philosophical level, but not perhaps the most helpful observation at the moment."

"There is nothing that ties us here any longer, Oliver. We can go anywhere we wish," said Ruadhan. "Perhaps even find a place where we can live as we wish. Antioch? The Isle of Cyprus? Maybe even Constantinople itself?" Ruadhan's eyes shone brightly.

"Your excitement is contagious," grinned Oliver. "If I have learned anything since I left Acre – and I like to think I have – it is that I need someone to follow, and that the same person I follow also needs to follow me. Call that what you will. But you, Ruadhan Ui Neill, are going to show me the world and all its wonders. And I am going to follow you."

"Sounds like I have my marching orders," said Ruadhan, smiling as he felt all his worries and burdens lifting. His heart felt as if it would burst from happiness.

"Do you hear that, Simon?" called Oliver lightly. "We're going to see the world."

"God works in mysterious ways, milord," came his servant's reply.

## About the Author

Tom has been in love with stories his entire life, and now he's finally creating them!

He started writing in order to be able to read the sort of stories he wanted.

With Tom's love of romantic stories (sometimes with a dark edge to them), he wanted to explore the possibilities of mixing classic themes with ideas that are close to him as a person. So far, he has explored a few different types of romance, and likes to blend romance with excitement and adventure.

Tom invites you to come and escape with him into the

worlds he makes - some are entirely his, and some might look similar to things you already know!

Milton Keynes UK
Ingram Content Group UK Ltd.
UKHW020843081124
450926UK00013BA/829

9 781965 514078